The Haunting of Grey Cliffs

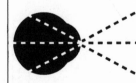

This Large Print Book carries the
Seal of Approval of N.A.V.H.

The Haunting of Grey Cliffs

Nina Coombs Pykare

Thorndike Press • **Thorndike, Maine**

Published in 2000 by arrangement with
Maureen Moran Agency.

Thorndike Large Print® Romance Series.

The tree indicium is a trademark of Thorndike Press.

The text of this Large Print edition is unabridged.
Other aspects of the book may vary from the original edition.

Set in 16 pt. Plantin by Al Chase.

Printed in the United States on permanent paper.

Library of Congress Cataloging-in-Publication Data
Pykare, Nina.
    The haunting of Grey Cliffs / Nina Coombs Pykare.
        p.   cm.
    ISBN 0-7862-2350-2 (lg. print : hc : alk. paper)
    1. Cornwall (England) — Fiction.   2. Large type books.
    I. Title.
    PS3566.Y48 H38 2000
    813'.54—dc21   99-054474

For my mother,
who taught me about love

Chapter One

I looked into the brooding eyes of the stranger, eyes set in a dark, handsome face. The thing he had just suggested was inconceivable, preposterous. The very idea quite took my breath away.

"Milord," I said, willing my voice to a steadiness I wished to feel and yet could not. "I cannot marry you, a man I have only just met, a total stranger."

Edward, Earl of Grey Cliffs, fixed me with those brooding eyes, eyes as black as pitch and revealing just as little. He sat across the small table from me in the private parlor of the inn where I had come in response to his message.

"I am not a total stranger, Miss Durant," he pointed out, his deep voice carrying the authority of a peer of the realm. "You will recall that I come to you with the recommendation of the marquis of Carolington."

This was true, in a rather roundabout fashion. Actually, the marquis had recommended *me* to the earl. I had earned a reputation for dealing with boys, especially young scamps who delighted in driving off their governesses. The earl had such a son — Andrew by name — and the earl and I had spent the last hour discussing him and his problems. The boy did need me; I could tell that. And I was more than ready to undertake his education.

I had come to this interview prepared to be offered employment as a governess. But this! I had not come expecting a proposal of marriage!

"Milord," I protested, "there must be many ladies in London more appropriate to hold the position of your wife. I am only a governess."

The earl straightened in his chair. "I am well aware of your qualifications," he said, his voice stringent. "And as to the ladies of London —" His handsome face twisted into a harsh imitation of a smile I found more frightening than any frown. "The ladies of London hold no charm for me. I have no wish to ally myself with any — lady."

The last word was uttered with great bitterness. I was no stranger to pain and it was pain I recognized beneath the man's acrimonious tone. The personable lineaments of his face — and they were personable despite his obvious anger — did not hide a certain anguish.

Having always a heart easily affected by

suffering, I felt some sympathy for the earl, but sympathy was very different from love. And I, when I had thought of marriage, had thought always of love.

I knew that many — perhaps most — ladies in that year of 1817 married not for love but for monetary reasons, but I was not the sort to think of money in relation to a man.

The earl was still regarding me, his dark eyes hooded, his handsome face now devoid of all expression. A frisson of fear slithered down my spine. Perhaps, I thought, dismissing the shiver, someone had trod on my grave. I could see no occasion for fear in this situation. The earl was an honorable man; the marquis had vouched for him.

"I understand that this has been somewhat of a jolt for you," the earl commented. "I am sorry for that. I had no intention of causing you distress."

He seemed to grow bigger as his eyes bore into mine, bigger and even more imposing. "Take your time, Miss Durant. Ask any questions you wish."

Questions! I hesitated, smoothing at the skirt of my drab brown gown with nervous fingers. How was I to ascertain which question to ask the man first? And then I realized what I most needed to know.

"Milord." My voice squeaked slightly and I firmed my shoulders to show I was in control of myself. "Since you give me permission, I *will* ask. Why me? Why should *I* be chosen as the object of your matrimonial intentions?"

The earl smiled, sadly this tune. He flicked a piece of lint from his well-fitting coat. "You are quite as intelligent as the marquis made you out to be," he declared. "And certainly I will tell you why I have chosen you. But first, relax a little, have some tea. And be assured I shall soon satisfy all your objections."

I did not see how that could be possible — my mind was such a riot of objections — but nervousness had dried out my mouth. So I took up my cup for a welcome sip of tea.

The earl leaned his elbows upon the table and looked me in the eye. "The marquis assured me you were the one to deal with Ned's unruliness and now that I have talked with you myself I am persuaded of it."

"I know how to deal with boys," I said, returning his look over the rim of my cup. "But I do not know how to deal with a proposal that I become a countess." Not that I should really consider such an outlandish suggestion, but the man had asked for a chance to present his case. Common courtesy dictated that I at least listen to him. "I know little about life in the ton."

"First," he said, "you may rest easy on that score. I do not intend that we shall go about in society."

I supposed he meant it at that moment, but I did not see how any lord would long wish to forego the joys of society. And when he returned to them, I didn't fancy being put down by the ladies of the ton. I was, in fact, well-born myself, but Jeremy's death in Spain — Jeremy, my dearly loved younger brother and Papa's only son — had so deranged Papa that he had lost all regard for the estate, an estate that would eventually go to a distant relative upon whom it was entailed.

I did not blame Papa that in his derangement he had also forgotten about me. I, too, had grieved deeply, but Papa died leaving me bereft of family and funds — so that in the end it was my love for Jeremy that proved my salvation from abject poverty. Because I had raised Jeremy from an infant I knew how to deal with boys. And because I knew how to deal with boys I was able to get employment as a governess.

The earl had picked up his teacup and was regarding me over the rim of it, and I realized that he must think he had answered my objections. I hastened to let him know otherwise. "But in future," I said, "you may well change your mind and wish to return to society."

The earl sighed, a sound of great distress. "I did not wish to bother you with all the sordid facts," he began.

There was anger in his tone, in his expression — anger and something more. "Milord," I interrupted, experiencing a tremor of trepidation. "You need not tell me —"

"I fear I *do* need," he said, setting his cup down on the table with a thump. "I have asked you to be my wife and you have every right to know the reputation of the man who has asked for your hand. My reputation is — in a word — quite bad."

"Bad?" I repeated, dismayed to hear the quaver in my voice.

He straightened his shoulders. "Quite so. It happened in this wise. My first wife, Royale, was a beautiful woman, a very beautiful woman." He paused and a look of unutterable misery cast a pall across his features. "Unfortunately, her beauty was only skin deep."

I felt a slight flush climb to my cheeks. Though I knew myself far from ugly, I had never set up to be a beauty. My hair, though luxuriant when released from its governess's Spartan knot, was an ordinary brown, and my eyes an ordinary green.

Charles had thought me beautiful, or at least he'd said he had, but Charles had been dead these five years, killed in the same battle as Jeremy. That power-mad Frenchman, Napoleon Bonaparte, had taken from me both husband-to-be and brother — and a year later, from his grief, my father.

"My wife," the earl continued, "did not want a child and resented the removal from society that its impending arrival made necessary."

My hands commenced to tremble and hastily I returned my cup to its saucer. What sort of barbarous woman did not want her own child? Many a night, alone in my narrow governess's bed, I had mourned the children I would never have. Charles had been my first love and he had been my last — and when poverty forced me to become a governess I knew that I should never marry.

The earl had fallen into a reverie, a painful one from the look on his face. I waited some minutes and then I asked, "What happened, milord?"

He started and smiled at me grimly. "After the child was born, she retaliated by

13

making me the laughingstock of London, cuckolding me with every man she could find. And then she ran off to the colonies — with a footman."

My shock must have registered on my face in spite of all my efforts to hide it.

"Yes," he said, his voice vibrating with fury. "With a footman! I stayed in the city." His face took on the look of granite, hewn to angular lines by time and adversity. "For two years I attended every social function to which I was invited, facing down every innuendo, every smirking matron, every prying fop." He frowned ferociously. "The talk died down finally and I found the so-called delights of the city no longer appealed to me. So a year ago I removed, as I told you, to my castle in Cornwall."

It was all rather confusing, but one thing was obvious — the earl was a proud man, this scandal had tried him sorely.

He gave me a strange speculative look. "If you require to be in the city," he said, leaning across the table toward me, "I could reconsider my decision."

"Oh no! Cornwall, Cornwall will be fine. That is —" I stammered on, not wanting him to construe my words as an acceptance of his proposal. "I do not care to live in London." My tongue seemed unable to obey my commands, or perhaps my thoughts were so jumbled they made little sense. I forced myself to take a deep breath. "Milord, please forgive me, I am all confused."

"How so?" he asked, his tone kindly.

"I cannot see why I must be your wife to care for —"

"The boy needs love," he interrupted harshly. "He adored his mother, though she had little time for him."

"But I *will* — that is, I would love him," I insisted. "Marriage is not necessary for that."

He shook his head stubbornly. "I think it is. I want the boy to have someone steady, someone solid to hang on to."

Still I did not understand. "But he has you, milord. He has his father."

A shadow crossed his face. "True, but if we marry, he will also have you." He paused and his face darkened further. "If you accept my suit," he said, "I intend to name you in my will as the boy's guardian."

Again a premonition of danger shivered over me. "Milord, you talk like a man who may not —" I could not finish the sentence. To think of this great strong man at death's door was frightening. "Are you ill?"

"No, no. It is nothing like that." He af-

15

fected a smile, but it did not reach his eyes, which remained black as a moonless midnight. "Life is chancy," he explained. "An accident while riding, a sudden swift illness . . . the boy has suffered much already. That's why I want a mother for him, not a governess who may depart on any whim."

It seemed unkind to remind him that marriage had not prevented the boy's real mother from departing, so I remained silent.

It was almost as though the earl read my mind; he leaned toward me further still, his strong mouth twisting in a sardonic smile. "You are not at all like her," he said. "She was fair and blonde, with all the dazzle — and hardness — of diamonds, but you, you are softness, calm, the peace of midnight."

I did not feel at all peaceful, and for a brief moment I actually envied the unhappy creature who had run off and left her child. It was only for a moment and only because when he spoke of her a peculiar look of longing stole over the earl's saturnine features.

"I know that Cornwall is a lonely place, removed from much society," he continued. "But from what the marquis told me I thought that would not be amiss with you."

This was all madness, I thought, trying to

control emotions as unruly as any I had ever contended with among my charges. How could I marry a stranger? How could he?

"You — you know only what the marquis told you of me," I went on, hesitantly, playing devil's advocate. "How can you wish to spend your life with me on such short acquaintance?"

"I know more about you than you think," he returned, his gaze never wavering. "I, too, served in Spain. I knew Jeremy — and Charles."

My heart almost leaped out of my throat. "You knew Jeremy? You knew my brother?"

He nodded, for the first time smiling warmly. "Many a bivouac your brother enlivened with his tales of snakes in your bed and toads in your dresser drawers, the numerous escapades of his mischievous youth."

"You knew Jeremy," I repeated, hardly able to comprehend it.

"He spoke of you always with great affection," the earl said, reaching across the little table to cover my hand with his. His fingers were warm, comforting, and to my surprise I did not resent the liberty he took in touching me.

For a long moment he remained with his hand over mine, then he withdrew it and to my consternation I experienced a sense of loss. It was because of Jeremy, I told myself briskly, because I was still missing Jeremy.

"Have you any more questions?" the earl inquired.

I shook my head, unable to speak over the lump in my throat, the lump that rose when I thought overmuch of Jeremy being gone.

"I realize I have given you a great deal to contemplate," the earl said. "Perhaps you would like some time to consider all this."

I nodded, reaching in my reticule for a handkerchief.

"So," he went on, "I shall repair to that chair over by the fire." His eyes searched my face. "If you have any more questions or if you wish to indicate conditions, something more than I have offered —"

I shook my head so violently that he smiled again. "Very well, I shall leave you to your decision making."

He got to his feet, and I should have been blind had I not seen that he was a fine figure of a man, broad-shouldered, lean-hipped, with the look of one who has led an active outdoor life, and yet as well dressed as even Beau Brummel could require.

The earl crossed the parlor to the fire, sank into a worn leather chair, and stretched his gleaming boots toward the grate.

A husband, I thought, trying to collect my rioting thoughts. How incredible! If I liked, I might have a husband — and not just any husband but a handsome, titled one, with a castle in Cornwall.

My practical nature asserted itself then and began to insist that I *think*. In spite of his having been friend to Jeremy, I knew very little of the earl. What kind of husband would he make? That first wife, that Royale, she had not thought him much of a husband. But then, she had not been much of a wife. I shivered in my chair though the room was warm. The earl had looked quite ferocious when he spoke of the footman. No wonder the two had left the country.

Why had she disliked her husband so? And how could she have forsaken her child? But there were no answers to such questions.

Enough speculation on the earl's first wife, I told myself. I would never know why she had done what she'd done, but her behavior and her reasons for it were not my problem. My problem was that I must decide if I wished to be his second wife.

I set myself to examining both sides of the question, a trick learned from Papa in his better days.

What had I to consider here? First, the

place. Removal to Cornwall was of little moment to me. I had no desire for the amusements of high society or the excitement of life in the city. I had always loved the country and could be quite happy there. So *place* would go on the "Good" side of my mental ledger.

Second, there was the child Ned, who from what his father had said was in dire need of a woman's love. As always, a new child to work with made me feel an expectancy much like that of a hunter riding to hounds — or so I imagined since I did not ride. I had shared my brother's fascination for frogs and toads, snakes and field mice, but I drew the line at horses. Not even my beloved Jeremy could persuade me to trust one of those wild creatures whose mad runaway had left us both motherless. But I would not need to ride, so the horses could be forgotten. The boy, too, went on the "Good" side.

Third, there was the earl himself, a personable man, concerned for his son, kind to me. As good a man as any — if I had to wed a stranger.

And fourth — A blush rose to my cheeks and spread over my entire body as my mind finally allowed me to comprehend that my heart's desire, the secret longing of many years, was actually within my reach. If I married the earl, I might have a child of my own!

The thought brought fresh tears to my eyes, which, because he had considerately turned his back on me to afford me more privacy, the earl did not see.

A child of my own, a sweet babe to hold in my arms, to call me Mama. The picture was so enchanting I could almost see the child. Dark it would be, dark like its father — and me.

I looked down at my hands, clutching my tear-dampened handkerchief in my lap. Within the year those hands might hold my child. Not since Charles's death had I thought . . . nor even dared to pray. . . . A little sob escaped my throat, a small sound scarcely louder than a twig crackling in the fire, yet the earl was on his feet, his face turned to me questioningly.

I swallowed, looking up at him. "I find, milord, that I have one more question."

"Of course," he said, advancing toward me. "Ask it."

I could not ask with him towering over me, so I got to my feet and stood trembling. "I . . ." I felt the blood rush to my face, but I must know before I could reach a decision. "This . . . this marriage between us . . . you

21

did not say . . ." I faltered to a halt. He waited, and finally I managed to go on. "You did not say if it was to be — be consummated."

His features hardened into a frown. "I'm sorry," he said gravely, "but I cannot agree to a marriage in name only."

Evidently he did not hear my sigh of relief, his somber expression did not lighten. "You see," he continued, "I find myself also in need of love and affection." He touched my cheek lightly, his fingers warm. "And I had hoped you might learn to give it to me."

A certain tenderness possessed me, perhaps because I was thinking of what he might give *me* — the child of my dreams. "I cannot promise you love," I said, my voice breaking. "But certainly I can give you affection. And when you are the father of my child —"

I saw recognition dawn in his eyes — and then a kind of cold bleakness gathering there. "I understand," he said, his voice gone chill. "You marry me so you may have a child of your own."

He took a step back, as though he no longer cared to be that near me. "I should have realized," he said, his tone acid. "Each woman has her price."

He made me sound so mercenary, so hard. "Milord —" I wanted to explain, but he cut me off with a sharp motion of his hand.

"Never mind, Miss Durant. At least it is a price I can pay." He gave me a severe look. "Just see that you have love enough left for Ned."

The sharpness of his tone shocked me into indignation. "Of course I shall! As I love God, I give you my solemn oath, I shall love and care for Ned as if he were my own flesh and blood."

The earl sighed, his expression unreadable, his eyes clouded. "I suppose I can ask for no more than that."

Chapter Two

And so the next morning the earl and I set forth for Cornwall. I was wearing my best blue silk, my hooded cloak that had seen better days, and my one and only bonnet. Staring down at the plain gold band on my finger, I was sore put not to imagine myself dreaming. But surely this was too much for any dream — to meet a man one day and wed him the next, setting out immediately for his castle and a son that I had never seen. It was foolhardy, this swift action I had taken. I knew it was foolhardy, and yet, settled beside my new husband in his fashionable carriage, with the lap robe tucked neatly over my knees, I did not even consider the reckless nature of my actions.

It was, perhaps, just as well, for had I had any presentiment of what the future was to bring me, I might well have beaten a hasty retreat and remained a spinster for the rest of my life.

But that morning as I watched the English countryside unfold before me in all its autumn splendor, I gave little thought to the icy frost of winter that was soon to follow or what, besides a new son, might await me in Cornwall.

The earl, now that he had achieved his purpose and acquired the mother he wished for his son, had lost a little of his sternness, and he left me to my own devices, not attempting to draw me into conversation but staring out the window as though he had much on his mind.

I appreciated his thoughtfulness, but after we had ridden some time I grew tired of my own company and turned to him. "Tell me, please, about my new — about Ned."

He nodded. "He was always a good child, as an infant happy and cheerful."

I liked the sound of that. I held that a child was born with a disposition that would be revealed in his character. If Ned's basic disposition tended to be cheerful, my task would be the easier. I did think of it as a task, but not in any pejorative fashion. My love for my charges had always run deep, and I believed Ned would soon hold his own place in my heart, a special place because he would be my son — and brother to the babe to come. Already, in that short space of time, the babe had become very real to me and occupied much of my thought.

"What does Ned like to do?" I asked the earl.

He smiled, I thought a trifle sadly. "These days he likes most to make mischief. He has driven away more governesses than I care to count, harassed them with any number of rascally tricks. So you can see why, when I ran into the marquis, I was about at my wits' end."

He patted my hand. "I cannot tell you how pleased I am that Ned will be in your hands."

I accepted the compliment with a nod. His touch made me feel strangely warm, but I disregarded that and continued with my questions. "Does Ned like the usual boy things?"

The earl wrinkled his dark forehead in thought. "Well, he likes to be outdoors, he likes the sea. We are close to the sea. He has a dog — Captain."

A peculiar change went over his face, almost as though he'd suffered some kind of pain "The dog belonged to my father and when he — died — suddenly, the boy took the dog as his."

A dog was good, I thought. It might give me a way to reach the boy.

The earl sent me a penetrating look. "Ned loves horses, he rides on the moors whenever he can."

My heart rose up in my throat and the

hands I held together in my lap trembled. I was not a fearful woman, but horses . . . I had nightmares still of the dreadful rearing horses, the sound of their pounding hooves, Mama clutching me to her as the carriage careened madly down the road, then the awful sensation of flying through the air, and the horrifying stillness of Mama's form when I crept to where she lay.

I knew it was not the fault of the horses. They were frightened into the mad gallop — by what we never knew. But still I feared the beasts who were responsible for the death of my beloved mother.

My face must have gone quite white, for the earl leaned toward me and covered my trembling hand with his. "Do not concern yourself, Hester," he said. "You needn't ride. The boy has been going out by himself for some time."

I scarcely heard the second part of his speech because I saw in his eyes that he had divined my secret, that he somehow knew about my fear of horses. "How —" I began.

He put an arm around my shoulders and I did not dislike the sensation, indeed, I found it comforting. "Jeremy and I spent many long, lonely nights waiting in camp. He talked of you and his childhood, and I talked of Ned, then only an infant."

I was very happy that my husband had known Jeremy. My brother was still so fresh in my memory. Not like my fiancé, Charles, who had become a hazy figure to me, almost a make-believe knight. But then, I had not known him long before our engagement nor had much opportunity to know him after.

Ours had been a whirlwind courtship. Jeremy brought Charles home with him on leave, and when they left Charles and I had an understanding. Then I did not see him again.

But Jeremy had long been the center of my life, to my heart almost *my* child, for it was I who had raised him, though only four years his elder.

I looked up at the earl. There seemed to be a sort of comfort in the sable eyes so near my own. "You are very kind," I said.

To my amazement the earl laughed, a rough discordant sound. "Let us only hope you continue to think so," he murmured, his face averted.

I thought that a strange thing to say to a new bride, even one wed under the peculiar circumstances of our union, but I did not pursue the matter for I found myself suddenly quite exhausted.

We had been driving already for a long time and the strangeness of the day before's

28

interview and the excitement of the morning's marriage now seemed to catch up with me. I yawned, covering my mouth with my hand.

"You are weary," he said "Why don't you nap a little? You will find you may lean against me quite comfortably."

And, indeed, I was quite comfortable. As the carriage drew ever nearer Cornwall and the castle that was to be my home, I slept in the arms of a man who, the day before, had been an utter stranger to me. I slept and dreamt of my child — our child — smiling up at me from my lap.

When I woke sometime later and looked up into my husband's eyes, I felt strangely warm there in his arms and more than a little flustered. Then, as I realized that my hand lay quite familiarly on his hard-muscled thigh, I straightened in embarrassment and drew it back.

He did not comment, nor could I tell from his face if he had even noticed.

We talked more then, as acquaintances might, of the estate and the village near Grey Cliffs, of Ned's childhood pranks, and of the time my husband had spent in Spain and his talks with Jeremy.

And finally, just as dusk was falling, Grey

Cliffs came into view. The earl had the driver stop the carriage so I might descend and look up at my new home.

My husband helped me down and I stood staring. I had expected a castle — he had told me a castle — but I had not expected this great fortress of grim, dark stone silhouetted against the somber sky. Situated on the top of the cliffs from which it took its name, the castle brooded like some great leviathan contemplating the extinction of mankind.

A single light shone from one window high up. The rest were dark, making the place look even eerier.

I quieted my pounding heart. The castle only looked so foreboding, I told myself, because the earl had been absent from it. Together we would make it a place of warmth, of happiness. We *would,* I told myself.

The road up to the castle twisted between stunted oaks, part of a wood that encompassed it on three sides. "The trees," I murmured. "Why are they so small, so twisted? They almost look like they are in torment."

My husband turned to me, his face grim. "The storms from the sea are fierce in winter. The trees are battered severely, but they manage to survive."

I glanced up at him. His jaw was set in a

hard line. Was he thinking of the storms of scandal *he* had survived?

At that moment the wind picked up, buffeting my cloak, tugging at my clothes like a living thing, a malignant living thing. The wind was cold, but even colder was the dismal aspect of the castle that was to be my home.

The earl helped me back into the carriage and settled beside me. His face looked drawn and I wondered if he worried about Ned's reaction to a new mother. Impulsively I leaned toward him and, copying the gesture of comfort he had used earlier, I covered his hand with mine. "It will be all right," I assured him. "I know children. Ned will come round."

"He hardly speaks to me," the earl muttered miserably. "He's so wild, so distant. He needs your help."

He turned to me, grasping me by the shoulders, gazing at me in a kind of desperation. "Hester, please, swear to me by all that you hold holy that you will love my son, stand by him —"

I thought he was worrying again about my leaving them, or about my loving our child more than Ned. So I looked directly into his eyes and said, "I swear to you by all that I hold holy that I will never desert Ned, that he will be to me a son, *my* son." It was an honest promise, honestly given, but I had no idea what the keeping of it would cost me.

My husband released my shoulders, his features relaxing a little.

As the carriage made its way up the winding road, night fell. The darkness prevented me from seeing the stunted oaks through which we were passing, but the gloom seemed to press in through the windows, filling the carriage with a despair almost tangible.

And then the carriage stopped. "We are home," the earl said.

He handed me down, and as we made our way up the walk toward the door the moon came from behind a cloud. Its light should have been welcome, but it only added to the eeriness of the scene, causing the oaks to throw threatening, contorted shadows around us like so many elusive demons let loose from the nether regions.

I shivered and drew closer to my husband. I had expected trouble, but I had expected it to come in the shape of frogs, snakes, spiders — a boy's idea of frightening — not this aura of impending disaster, of unseen evil hovering at my heels.

As we approached it, the great oaken door

swung slowly open. The interior of the castle was dark and for a moment it seemed that the door had opened of its own volition. But I had not weathered so many boys' tricks for nothing. I had strong nerves, and my steps did not falter nor my hand tremble upon my husband's arm.

And then as we drew closer, I saw that the door had not opened by itself. A butler stood there in the gloom, dressed entirely in black. A gaunt man, his features pinched, his face expressionless, he moved like one just raised from the dead.

"Welcome home, milord," he said in tones that conveyed no feeling whatsoever.

My husband didn't seem to notice. We stepped inside, and as the great door started to swing shut behind us I had to battle a strong urge to break and run, back out into the threatening moonlight, down between the twisted gnarled oaks, as fast as I possibly could, all the way back to London.

Of course, I did not run. I stood still and looked around me. The interior of the castle was even grimmer than the outside. Candelabras were stationed along the walls, but their flickering light was feeble and the place dismally chill. True, a fire burned on the great hearth, but it was a small fire and the entry hall was huge — no doubt knights in armor had once ridden their chargers up the hill and in through the front door. To tell the truth, I would have welcomed a knight, even on horseback — anything to relieve the awful melancholy of the place.

Then I straightened my shoulders and reminded myself that God had answered my unspoken prayers, that I now had a definite purpose — I was meant to bring love to this dismal place, love and a new little life. I would remember that, I told myself, the new little life.

"So," said my husband, his dark gaze searching mine. "What do you think?"

Mama had taught me that if I couldn't say something nice I should say nothing at all, but that would not serve here with my husband so clearly awaiting a reply.

I moistened my dry lips. "It is . . . it is very big," I ventured.

And my husband broke into laughter and hugged me to him.

It was a very confusing moment for me as a riot of unexpected feeling erupted inside me. Five years had dimmed the memory of the sensations I had experienced in caring for Charles, but I did not recall ever feeling such unexpected warmth or the strange desire I now had to burrow into my husband's waistcoat and beg to stay close to him.

Of course he released me and of course I did not beg to be held close again, but the experience heartened me. Since I did not find being near my husband upsetting, nay, found it very pleasant, the begetting of our child should come more easily.

All of this passed through my mind quite quickly, while the earl's laughter still rang through the great hall.

Then out of the darkness came a quavering voice, which, in spite of its feebleness, carried sharp condemnation. "Such levity is unseemly," it said. "Your father will not like it."

I started and looked up at the earl. "You said —"

"I said my father is dead," he replied sternly. "And he is. Cousin Julia, quit lurking about in the shadows and come meet my new wife."

"The year of mourning is not up," Cousin Julia said querulously. "You should not be marrying."

The earl slipped an arm around my waist and I admit to relishing its warmth. "The boy needs a mother," he said. "Hester will be good for him."

The words were about the boy and yet underlying them I seemed to hear something else, an unspoken plea — and I remembered him saying so seriously to me that he, too, needed love and affection. And in that moment I wanted to give them to him. Smiling, I leaned a little closer into his warmth and strength. "Good evening, Cousin Julia," I said to the vague shape just emerging from the shadows. "How kind of you to come to visit."

Because I was close to him, the length of my side against his, I felt the slight stiffening of the earl's body. "Cousin Julia lives with us," he said, his voice devoid of emotion.

I fixed a smile on my face, reminding myself that the castle was the earl's; he was its lord and had the right to provide homes for any relatives he chose, even this old woman who, now that I could see her, looked as though her principal occupation in life was stuffing herself with anything edible.

Cousin Julia's bright blue eyes gazed at me above cheeks that swelled out like two great rounds of unbaked bread and looked about as puffy. "You're the new wife," she said, nodding sagely. "The earl said you were coming."

I turned to my husband. "How could you say that? You didn't know I would accept."

"Not him," Cousin Julia said in disgust, her face wrinkling up so that her eyes all but disappeared. "His father."

"But —" I was thoroughly bewildered. "Your father is dead."

The earl nodded gravely, but Cousin Julia ignored me. "Just last night," she continued in that quavering voice that contrasted so oddly with her bulk, "your father was telling me —"

A violent fit of trembling overtook me. What kind of woman was this who thought she could speak with the dead?

My husband drew me closer still. "You are chilled," he said. "Come nearer the fire. Hillyer, bring us some hot tea — and something to eat with it."

"Yes, milord."

The butler disappeared into the gloom and the earl led me toward the hearth and several great chairs grouped around it. The fire's warmth was welcome but it did not reach far enough into the great damp room to do anyone much good.

"I believe I'll have a spot of tea myself," Cousin Julia said and plopped herself down on one of the chairs. In an effort to bring myself back to my usual sane sensibility I set myself to making an inventory of her person. She did not look like a madwoman, but neither did she look like a lady. She was short, perhaps five feet, no more, and very round. She wore a gown of some ugly shade of yellowish-green — in the firelight it was difficult to tell its exact color, though it was easy enough to see that the gown should have been larger. Her hair she had powdered and piled high on her head in an elaborate style much favored in the previous century. Evidently no one had told her that ladies no longer wore wigs or the enormous panniers that made her look as round as she was high.

My husband drew a chair closer to the fire for me and, feeling quite weary, I settled into it gratefully, clutching my cloak tighter around me.

Cousin Julia peered at me from her little eyes. "If someone you love is dead," she said, as calmly as she might have mentioned it was raining outside, "I can reach them for you."

"Reach?" My mind refused to consider this possibility, and yet my heart cried for Jeremy!

The earl put another chair beside mine and sank into it. "Cousin Julia has lately been studying the spiritualists," he explained. "They believe that the spirits of the dead may be contacted. By some people at least." His tone, too, was conversational, as though he thought such chicanery actually possible.

"But —" I began.

"However," he went on smoothly, "should you choose to let *your* dead rest in peace, she will respect your wishes. Will you not, Cousin Julia?"

His voice did not change, did not lose its conversational tone, yet the threat was there, not to be ignored.

Cousin Julia heard it and nodded glumly. "Yes, yes. But it really is a great opportunity, my dear. The dead are so enlightened. They can tell us much, divulge such knowledge."

"Knowledge?" A deep voice came booming out of the darkness. "The best knowledge comes from old Lucifer, Beelzebub himself. Just wait till I call him up! Then we can know anything we want!"

Chapter Three

The great hall was quiet for the space of some seconds and I considered the possibility that I had arrived not at a castle but at a madhouse. Then a little man walked out into the firelight. He was about the same height as Cousin Julia, but that was the only resemblance between them. Where Cousin Julia was round, this man was thin, thin as a sapling. It would take six of him to make a Cousin Julia.

And while she was dressed in the fashion of some forgotten court, his clothes were of no particular time or style. What I could see of them, that is, under what appeared to be a heavy layer of dust.

He looked, indeed, as though he'd absentmindedly put on whatever items came first to his hand. His drab breeches were old and shabby, sagging at the knees and waist; his stockings were dropping. His bottle-green jacket was threadbare to the point of frayed elbows and missing buttons. His shirt more closely approached grey than white and to this was added a waistcoat of the most garish puce, shot through with threads of silver and gold that hung here and there in frayed strands. All in all, he was an incredible sight.

And then he spoke — and in my nervous anxiety I almost burst into hysterical laughter. For this little man, who seemed to have hardly the frame to support his shabby clothing, had a voice that boomed through the huge entry hall, a voice deep and sonorous. "So, Edward," he said, "you return successful."

My husband nodded. "Yes, Uncle Phillip. I was successful. Hester has become my wife."

"Good, good." Uncle Phillip crossed to me, tripping over his ill-fitting carpet slippers and almost falling at my feet. He righted himself just in time, took my hand in his, and pumped it with much more power than one would expect from such a wizened-looking man. "This place needs a woman's touch," he said heartily before he took the last empty chair. "Glad to have you here."

I inferred from the hard look Cousin Julia sent him that he had been taking a gibe at her, but I had little time for such speculations. In spite of this, the first even half-genuine welcome that I had received in my new home, I was feeling quite put out with my new husband.

I turned to him. "Uncle Phillip lives with us, too?" I asked, and I felt I might be forgiven for the touch of asperity that crept into my voice.

My husband looked a little surprised. Did he think I would *expect* a castle full of relatives? "Yes," he said, his tone soothing. "Uncle Phillip is my father's brother."

"I see," I replied. And then I decided it was time to ask yet another question, one I should perhaps have asked before I ever consented to come to this place. "And who else lives with us?" I asked with some acerbity.

Uncle Phillip laughed, a deep booming sound that fit his voice but not his person. "Should have told her everything, my boy. Don't treat her like your father would have. New brides are inclined to be touchy, you know." And Uncle Phillip winked at me.

I managed to smile back at him. At least he was friendly. But what had he meant talking so familiarly about the devil? Still, Uncle Phillip seemed more eccentric than evil; perhaps he was just amusing himself at my expense.

My husband had not answered me and I turned in my chair again to give him another questioning look.

He merely shrugged. "I have a younger brother, Robert. Sometimes he stays here — temporarily."

Uncle Phillip chuckled. " 'Temporarily' means till Robert's quarterly allowance comes due again and he can go back to London and the high life he enjoys."

The earl didn't look embarrassed at Uncle Phillip's forthright comments. "My uncle is right. But Robert should give you no problems." A strange expression crossed his face. "That is, if you know enough to disregard his womanizing ways."

From the look on my husband's face, he found his brother's rakish behavior annoying in the extreme.

"So," I said with a sigh of resignation, "that comprises the entire household?"

The earl's nod of agreement was interrupted by Cousin Julia's cackling chuckle. Both he and I turned to her with surprise. "Now what?" the earl asked angrily. My husband had a temper, I thought — a temper rather too easily aroused.

Cousin Julia smirked, there was no other word for it, her eyes almost disappearing into her fat cheeks. "Not quite all. They came yesterday."

"They? Who are they?" the earl demanded with scant patience. "My God, woman, enough!" He leaped to his feet and strode to her chair, towering over her. "Who did my brother bring home this time? If it's some village girl —"

"The twins," Uncle Phillip interrupted. "And it wasn't Robert brought them, it was their mother's brother."

"Why?" the earl snapped. "They have their money. For these seven years."

Cousin Julia tittered, setting my nerves on edge even more. "Of course," she said, "but now they are to live in the castle."

"Here!" The earl's face darkened. "That is impossible."

This was not making sense to me. Why should the earl refuse a home to his nephews? I turned to Uncle Phillip. "Why, if the twins have not lived here before, were they brought here now?"

"It doesn't matter," the earl shouted. "I'll not have Robert's illegitimate brats here in the castle!"

So that was it — Robert's twins had been born on the wrong side of the blanket. But they were not to be blamed for that. I turned —

"Their mother died," Uncle Phillip was saying calmly. "Taken off by the fever. There's no woman to care for them."

The earl stopped his stomping up and

down the hearth to frown. "Their uncle should have taken them somewhere else then."

"Milord." I, too, rose and moved until I could look up into his eyes, eyes now gone so hard, so cold. "Milord, your brother's sons —"

His face, frigid, glacial, seemed to belong to a stranger. Though I hadn't known him long, I had thought him a man of some kindness, but now — now I saw only a bitter, calloused man, a man who meant to throw his brother's children out into the cold.

His gaze did not waver, remaining chill as a winter dawn. My legs began to tremble, but I could not back down, not when the welfare of children was concerned.

The earl continued to stare at me, his eyes unblinking, his gaze hostile. "I do not believe I asked for your sentiments on the matter," he said.

I was brought quite suddenly to the awareness that I had overstepped my bounds. "I know you did not," I replied, willing my voice to calmness and trying for a placating tone; but my effort had no effect, the earl continued to stare at me in icy anger.

"These are children," I pointed out, my

own temper mounting. "Mere children. In no way can they be held responsible for their parentage." My tone matched his in iciness. "Children," I repeated.

For a moment I thought that his temper would explode at me. His jaw thrust out and a muscle on one side of his mouth twitched ominously. I could see that it was only with great force of will that he kept from cursing at me. But knowing I was in the right, I held my ground.

"My brother," he said, his voice stinging, "has illegitimate brats spread across the face of Cornwall, of England. Am I to support them all?"

I met his glare with one of my own. "Has anyone asked you to?"

Behind me, Cousin Julia cackled. For such an enormously fat woman she had an extremely shrill laugh. And that feeble yet vitriolic voice could soon wear on a person's nerves. As I turned toward her, she cackled again, the folds of fat beneath her chin quivering. Then she sobered. "Shall I ask your father —"

The earl whirled. "Forget my father! I am the earl now. *I* give the orders! Now, get out of here. Go to bed."

Cousin Julia shook her head at me, heaved herself to her feet, and waddled out.

If I had been less distressed, I might have found the sight amusing. As it was, I was quite beside myself. To think that the man would turn out innocent children — I had made a mistake, I thought, a horrible mistake. I should never have married in such haste. I did not want this coldhearted man to father my child.

But I knew myself fairly trapped. I had sworn a solemn oath on all I held holy, an oath more sacred to me than even my marriage vows, to love the boy Ned as my own son. I could not leave this place however much I might dislike it — or the man who was now my husband — without disregarding that holy oath.

I turned again to him, but he was advancing on Uncle Phillip, his face a thundercloud of anger. "Where are they?"

The old man did not blanch. Did that mean he was accustomed to the earl's tempers, that he experienced them often?

"We put them in the nursery," Uncle Phillip boomed.

"With Ned?" The earl groaned.

Uncle Phillip nodded. "I'm sorry, Edward. We just didn't know what else to do with them." He glanced toward the clock. "All in bed they are," he said. "The upstairs maid, Betty, has been taking care of them."

The earl frowned. "How did Ned behave when the twins arrived?"

Uncle Phillip shrugged. "The boy didn't like it a bit, those two taking over his territory so to speak, but he accepted it."

The great clock in the corner chimed the hour — ten o'clock. Uncle Phillip got to his feet and turned toward the stairs, his eyes twinkling. "I've got to go, got things to get ready for the witching hour." He grinned in my direction, tripped, and almost fell again. "Sorry, my dear. I'm a mite clumsy, always have been. Good night."

I watched Uncle Phillip go out and I bit my tongue to keep from calling him back. I found I did not want to be alone with my husband. He had some cause for his outbreak of temper, of course, but to blame innocent children, to make them suffer for the sins of their fathers . . . I was most disappointed in him.

Hillyer returned finally with the hot tea and some stale biscuits. I sighed. The kitchen was no better run that the rest of this place. It appeared that the whole castle needed looking after.

I sipped my tea and ate one biscuit. The earl took only tea. He watched me closely, and as I finished the last bite, he rose. "You must be tired," he said, his tone even. "I will show you to your rooms."

My reluctance must have shown on my face — I had never been good at hiding my feelings.

"Our rooms adjoin," he observed dryly.

He took a candelabra from the nearby table and lit the way. The stairs were wide, five, perhaps six people could climb them abreast, and now they seemed huge and somehow threatening. At the top of the stairs all lay in Stygian darkness. As I ascended, my elbow in my husband's grip, I shivered, almost drooping with exhaustion. The darkness seemed to be pressing in, sapping me of strength.

Then I straightened. I would not allow anything to stand in my way. Ned's welfare was to come first, of course. And after that — Perhaps I had misjudged my husband. Surely having to deal with such a family could make a man tense to the point of eruption. A man saddled with such an entourage deserved sympathy rather than reproach.

Cousin Julia could try anyone's patience; certainly she had already tried mine. And Uncle Phillip's desire to meet the devil face-to-face was more than unorthodox and made me distinctly uneasy. If it made me feel that way, how did it affect the earl, who was responsible for the man?

And brother Robert! The earl, who had already suffered through much scandal, must have been galled by his brother's dishonorable conduct.

The stairs were tall as well as wide and the hall that led to our chambers long and dark. So by the time we reached there I had enjoyed ample time to consider my circumstances and to make allowances for my husband's behavior. After all, I was his wife, with a duty to care for him.

The earl opened the door, his expression revealing nothing. "This is your chamber," he said. "The housemaid will have already put your things away."

When I spied my best nightdress laid out across the lavender cover, my knees began to quake. I wanted a child, but I was not at all sure I wanted the consummation that must come before it, especially now.

The earl's gaze slid over the nightdress, ignoring it and the blush that rose to my cheeks. "You should have everything you need. Tomorrow you may send to the village for whatever else you want."

I saw what he was about, talking to me normally, acting as though his display of temper downstairs had not even happened. And his calmness did alleviate my fears.

He stepped closer to me. "So you want a child," he said softly, reaching out to touch my cheek. His fingers were warm, gentle. My skin felt warm, too, as though his fingers had imparted some of their warmth to it.

I nodded, mesmerized by the heat I saw in his eyes. He was looking at me differently, his eyes hooded, his mouth curved into the beginning of a smile. He took another step toward me, put his hands on my shoulders, and drew me close.

I felt my limbs go weak. His presence was overpowering, it seemed to envelop me. And when he put one warm finger under my chin and tilted my mouth up for his kiss I did not protest.

His lips were warm and persuasive, and the strange feelings I had experienced with him before returned. He kissed me for a long time, tenderly, gently, and then he turned me slowly about and began to unhook my gown.

Away from the mind-numbing influence of his lips, I was able once more to think. "Milord," I whispered, "please reconsider. Don't throw those poor children out." His fingers had ceased working with my hooks and I hurried on, frightened by my own temerity but determined, too. "They will be good for Ned and —"

51

With a curse he spun me away from him. "Enough!" he cried, tearing angrily at his cravat. "You know nothing about these boys."

I faced him though my knees were quivering with weakness. "I know that they are children and I know that children need love."

He glowered at me, his chest rising and falling with the force of his anger, his face growing redder by the second. "A noble sentiment indeed," he cried finally. "But as it appears we will not be begetting your precious child this night, perhaps you had best get to your bed and rest. You'll need all your powers of love tomorrow." He laughed harshly. "All." And he stomped off into the adjoining room, slamming the door behind him.

I stood there, half out of my gown, and a great sigh escaped me, whether of relief or disappointment I couldn't be sure. At any rate it seemed clear that this was not to be my wedding night.

I finished getting undressed, donned my nightdress, and, blowing out the candle, climbed into the big bed. The sheets had the smell of the outdoors about them and that helped to calm me.

I started on my prayers, dozed off once,

woke to finish them, and then lay, staring into the darkness.

Nothing at Grey Cliffs Castle had been as I expected. I had come into a place inhabited by — the most charitable designation was eccentrics — a mountainous woman who lived in the past and spoke, or thought she spoke, to the dead; a bumbling old man who wished to meet the devil face-to-face and enjoyed preparing for the witching hour; a womanizing younger brother apparently intent on populating the countryside with his by-blows; and a husband whose temper and disposition were clearly not of the best. And I had yet to meet the child Ned. Living among these people it was no wonder he was into mischief. And these two new boys — if I could persuade my husband to let them stay on, it was I who would have the care of them.

I shivered. I had taken on quite an enormous task. I prayed God I would be equal to it.

Chapter Four

I slept, finally, and woke in the grey light of dawn, chilled to the bone. The great bed seemed vast and I felt almost lost in it. Huddling under the covers, I struggled to summon my usual cheery morning spirits, spirits that seemed reluctant to waken with the rest of me. But since I am by nature an optimistic person, by the time the sun was fairly up I had talked myself into a better state of mind.

Last night I'd been weary from the long trip, my nerves still on edge from so many unexpected happenings. Perhaps in the cheerful light of day the knowledge of Cousin Julia and Uncle Phillip, Robert and his sons, would all be more easily dealt with. And today I would meet Ned.

I was not anxious about that meeting; indeed, I looked forward to it. Whatever tricks Ned had planned for me — and I was sure he *had* planned some — I was equal to them. And when the boy realized that I truly cared for him, he would come round. I had won over boys before. I had all the necessary qualities: a good stomach and strong nerves, a lot of love, and considerable patience.

I washed and put on my gown of drab brown, not fitting for my new position in life no doubt, but my blue silk was my one good gown and for the moment I meant to save it.

As I finished fixing my hair, a knock came on the door to the hall. "Come in," I called.

The door swung open and a rosy-cheeked maid stood there, holding a tray. She looked so very normal that for a moment I wondered what she could be doing in this place. Then I smiled and motioned her in.

"Good morning, milady," she said, setting the tray on a little table near me. "I've brung you some nice hot tea. It can be chilling here of a morning."

I poured myself a cup. "Thank you —"

"Betty, milady, me name's Betty."

I seemed to remember the name. "You're the upstairs maid?"

She bobbed a curtsey. "Yes, milady."

"And it is you who takes care of the new boys?"

Her round face squeezed into a frown. "Aye, milady, and a wickeder pair I ain't never seen!"

"Wicked?" I repeated in amusement, sipping my tea.

"Aye. They talks to each other — in some

strange language can't no one else make head ner tail of." Betty's eyes grew round and her cheeks redder. " 'Tis the devil's own tongue!" she breathed fearfully.

I shook my head. "I think not, Betty. They are children, just mischievous children."

I could see that she was far from convinced, but being a respectful girl she did not contradict me.

I heard a door opening behind me and saw Betty's expression change. If anything, she looked even more frightened. She backed hastily away, mumbling, "If that'll be all, milady?"

"Yes, of course." As she hurried out, I turned to face my husband, a husband who had entered my room without the courtesy of a knock.

"Good morning," he said pleasantly. "I hope you slept well."

I stared. Of all that I had expected or imagined during the long hours of the night, this ordinary greeting had not figured in my thoughts. Was this to be the way of it? I wondered. No apologies, not even any reference to the unpleasantness of the previous night?

"Good morning," I replied. "I slept reasonably well."

"Fine. I'll see you in the breakfast room." And he was gone.

I put down my cup, picked up my shawl, and followed him.

The breakfast room faced the sea. From its tall, narrow windows I could see the waves breaking against the rocks below, throwing up great swells of spume, and the ocean, this morning a deep blue-green, sparkling in the sun.

The sideboard was loaded with food and I found myself ravenously hungry. I filled a plate and took it to the table. My new husband exerted himself to make pleasant conversation and the events of the previous evening began to fade from my memory.

When I had satisfied my hunger, I turned to him. "I am eager to meet Ned." I hesitated, my eyes searching his face.

"Please," Edward said, his dark face twisting into a frown, his voice caustic. "No more implorings on behalf of the motherless twins."

I still could not stop myself. "But —"

He raised a hand. "I understand your feeling for the motherless," he said. "But my major concern is Ned."

"The company of other children —" I dared.

"I know," he replied sardonically, "will be good for Ned."

I stared at him; could this possibly mean —

He rightly interpreted my questioning look. "I have reconsidered my decision," he told me, his face severe. "The twins may stay — for now."

"Thank you! Oh thank you!" I cried. "I knew you were a good man."

I felt as though *I* had received the reprieve. And perhaps I had, for I wanted the father of my child to be —

He scowled. "Just be sure Ned isn't slighted."

This time I didn't take offense. "He won't be, I assure you. He won't be at all!"

Moments later I stood outside the nursery door. "Hello," I cried, pushing it open and stepping in with a smile on my face. "How are you this morning?"

The boys were sitting at table, just finishing their porridge. They raised their heads, two fair, one dark. Edward's son was easily recognizable even without his difference in coloring from the twins. Ned's scowl was just like his father's.

"I am — Hester," I said, deciding to forego the rather spurious titles of mother and aunt. "I am here to take care of you. We're going to have great fun."

The twins grinned, evidently willing to give me a chance, but Ned's scowl deepened. "We don't want you here," he said. "Go home."

I was prepared for his hostility. "I am home," I said calmly. "I live here now."

Ned's face twisted. "You can't be my mother! She's gone."

I nodded. "I know. I don't want to be your mother." A slight lie, I thought, for the boy's sake. My heart had already gone out to him. "But I am your father's wife."

The twins looked at each other and murmured something I couldn't make out.

"It's not polite to whisper in company," I said. "Why don't you speak aloud?"

The boy did, but though the words consisted of recognizable sounds, they made no sense.

I laughed and clapped my hands. "I see," I cried. "You have your own private language. How grand!"

I glanced sideways at Ned. "I wish I had someone to share such a language with."

I saw the flicker of interest in the boy's eyes, but he masked it quickly and remained silent. "Oh well. Ned, I hear you have a dog. Where is he?"

"He's mine!" Ned said fiercely.

I pretended not to notice the fierceness. "Yes, I know. I just want to say hello to him. I love dogs."

Ned frowned. "He's not allowed up here."

"My goodness, that's too bad. What did he do?"

Ned's face turned crimson. "He didn't do anything. It was me. I put a snake in the last governess's bed."

"Really?" I pretended surprise. "And she didn't like it?"

Ned looked startled, as well he might. " 'Course not. Girls are scared of snakes and stuff like that."

"Not me. I like snakes."

The boy stared at me and the twins looked at each other and snickered.

"Well," I said, turning toward the door. "I just came in to say hello. We'll start lessons tomorrow. Today I want to explore the castle." I moved toward the door. "It would be more fun if I had someone to go with me, but I suppose you're all busy."

The twins looked at each other and without exchanging a word got to their feet.

Ned hesitated, then he rose too. "I'd better come along," he said. "This is a big castle, and dark. A stranger could get lost in here."

★ ★ ★

The castle was big and dark. Gloomy, too, but having the twins along helped to enliven things. Their cheerful grins were like sunshine in the dim halls and their babbling language, though I couldn't understand it, was rather like the music of a brook.

The castle was laid out in a great square with rooms around each side facing out and a huge courtyard enclosed in the middle. It was gloomy because the windows, set in walls two feet thick, were small and narrow and so did not let in much light.

Ned served as guide, pointing out each room, many of which seemed empty. In one particularly dingy corridor he lowered his voice dramatically. "This castle has secret passageways. And a priest hole."

He turned wide eyes on me. "Do you know what a priest hole is?"

I shook my head. "No, tell me." Let the boy show off a little.

His chest seemed to expand. "Long time ago we were all Catholics. This bad king —" He hesitated, but I did not supply the king's name. "This king said we couldn't listen to priests anymore. We had to get rid of them."

He scowled. "But some people wouldn't.

So they made secret rooms no one could find and they hid the priests there." He gave me a triumphant look. "And *that's* why they're called priest holes."

I looked suitably impressed. "You're very good at history, Ned. Very good."

The beginning of a smile tugged at his mouth. Then he frowned. "Yes, we have a priest hole, but if you find the way to go in, don't go there by yourself. You could get lost and end up nothing but dry bones!"

The twins looked very impressed, and I have to admit that my voice had a slight quaver as I asked, "Have you found these passageways yet?" The thought of a child lost in there was chilling.

Ned shook his dark head. "Not yet. But I will."

I felt it too soon to ask the boy for any promises concerning his safety and, besides, he sounded already warned by some adult. Those dire words about dry bones sounded more like Uncle Phillip than Ned's father. I could not imagine Cousin Julia considering bones of any value. It was the spirit she wished to contact. So she might find such passageways full of such possibilities.

"How very exciting!" I cried. "This must be a fun place to live."

All three of them stared at me. Then one

of the twins said, "Too dark" and the other said, "Too gloomy." I was relieved to know they also spoke English.

Ned snorted, his facing turning rosy at these insults to his home. "It's a castle. Castles are supposed to be dark and gloomy!"

Another piece of information gleaned from his elders, I thought.

When we had come full circle back to the nursery, Ned paused. "You're really married to my father?"

"Yes, Ned."

I braced myself for another fierce outburst. But instead he said, "And you really like snakes?"

I smiled. "I think they're fascinating creatures."

He frowned. "Then you won't be mad that I left one in your desk drawer."

"In the schoolroom?"

He nodded, obviously not daring to believe what he was hearing.

I smiled at him. "No, I'm not mad. What a lovely gift." I looked at the other boys. "Maybe we can make it a home in the nursery."

The twins' mouths gaped open. Ned looked stunned, then he rallied. "I don't . . . I don't think my father would like that. Besides, the snake might want to go home."

My heart leaped with joy at this evidence of the boy's concern for a dumb creature, even while I sighed at the echo of the boy's own longing for a secure home. "That's true," I agreed. "Perhaps we should just say hello to him and then take him outside, so he can go home."

Ned nodded. "I only brought him up here because I miss Captain."

I nodded, but I knew better. The boy had meant to drive me off as he had the others. And he undoubtedly had some other tricks left.

"I think I'll speak to your father about Captain," I mused. "The dog must miss you."

I saw the boy's lip quiver, but his voice was strong. "Yeah, I guess he does."

When I returned to the main part of the castle, I was much heartened. I was sure Ned was a normal boy, somewhat overset by his mother's desertion, but some love should straighten him out. The twins didn't seem to present a problem. They, too, were in need of love, but not so badly as Ned. After all, they had each other.

My husband, I was told, had departed on estate business, and since it was time for the noon meal I took myself to the dining room

64

— a great gloomy cavern with a vast table in the middle. Numerous candles in rows of candelabras along the walls could not relieve the gloom. I must speak to my husband, I thought, and see if we might take our meals in the breakfast room, which at least got some sun.

I moved toward the sideboard. My morning excursion had sharpened an appetite that was always healthy.

I had filled my plate and chosen a seat at one end of the great table when Cousin Julia came in. This morning she had not powdered her hair, which appeared to be almost orange, and she was wearing a gown of deep, deep red. The sight was rather hard on the eyes.

"So, there you are," she said. "Isn't this room marvelous? I can just feel the spirits hovering."

She piled a plate so full of food that I wondered she could carry it. Then she came to sit beside me. I could have wished for a little time to myself, time to consider what I had discovered about my new charges and to plan for the future, but short of repairing to my room I didn't know how to get it.

"You should feel his presence," Cousin Julia said round a mouthful of food. "That's *his* chair."

The food in my mouth turned to straw and I swallowed hastily, mumbling, "Whose?"

"The late earl. 'Twas a terrible thing."

"Death is always difficult to handle," I agreed, wondering if Cousin Julia ever spoke about more cheerful subjects.

"Oh, it wasn't his death," she said, cramming half a muffin in her mouth. "Manner of it."

I paused, my fork halfway to my mouth, my lunch forgotten. "I'm afraid I don't understand."

Her eyes grew round, her expression pitying. "You mean Edward didn't tell you?"

"He told me his father is dead."

Cousin Julia shook her head. "He didn't tell you!"

I was fast losing patience with this sort of thing. "Cousin Julia, if there is something you think I should know, will *you* please tell me?"

"The earl, the late earl, he didn't just die. He . . . he was found hanging from his chandelier. By his cravat."

I clamped my mouth shut tight to keep the food I had already eaten from escaping from my stomach. "He . . . he killed himself?"

"That's what the magistrate said."

There was something about Cousin Julia's tone of voice, about the way she looked at me that told me there was more.

"And —"

"But there's some people hereabouts that don't believe it."

"You mean —" A cold hand seemed to grip my throat, making it difficult for me to breathe.

Cousin Julia stared at me. "I mean there's some that think the old earl was murdered!"

"Murdered!" I could scarcely credit my ears. "But wouldn't the magistrate —"

Cousin Julia snorted, spraying the table with muffin crumbs in a most disgusting way. "Our magistrate's an old fool. Couldn't find his coat if he took it off."

So much for law and order, I thought. "But if there was a murder," I said, "wouldn't there be evidence?"

"Maybe. Unless the murderer covered it up." Cousin Julia gulped down some tea and looked me in the eye. "But let me ask you this — if it wasn't murder, then why is the old earl haunting the place?"

My stomach rolled completely over. "H-haunting?"

"That's right. He's been seen by the servants. I've seen him myself." She frowned, twisting her face into a tortured grimace. "I just don't understand why he won't tell me who did it."

"Perhaps he doesn't know," I said. Then I realized that she almost had me believing. "That is —"

Cousin Julia smiled. "That's it!" she cried, clapping her hands. "It must have happened while he was asleep. Thank you, my dear."

"But Cousin Julia — I don't believe in ghosts."

Cousin Julia chortled. "Perhaps not now . . . but later, when you have seen him, you will be a believer. Yes, you will."

Cousin Julia ate for some time, devouring more food than most people would consume in an entire day. Though my appetite had deserted me, I forced myself to chew and swallow. When her plate was half empty, Cousin Julia turned to me. "I suppose he didn't tell you about *her* either."

I swallowed a furious retort. Cousin Julia seemed the sort who liked to make people angry at each other. I didn't intend to give her that satisfaction. "If you mean the former countess, you are wrong. Edward told me about her."

Cousin Julia licked her lips, her eyes gleaming. "She was the talk of all London.

You must have heard of her."

I looked Cousin Julia right in the eye. "I'm afraid I was too busy with the marquis of Carolington's children to be listening to gossip."

Cousin Julia's mouth formed a round O. "You mean —"

I laughed. "You mean, Edward didn't tell you? Before he married me, I was a governess."

"A — a governess?"

"Yes. And proud of it."

That should keep her quiet for a while, I thought, and finding my appetite quite gone, I repaired to my room to consider the happenings of this extraordinary day.

Chapter Five

Though my room was nicely appointed and relatively cheerful because large windows had been set into the thick stone walls, I was not able to enjoy the pleasantness of the room or the lovely view of the sea below it, now sparkling in the midday sun.

Murdered! The old earl had been murdered! Or so Cousin Julia believed.

Angrily I paced the length of the rug and back again, my temper flaring higher than the flames on the hearth. Another thing my fine new husband had neglected to tell me!

But who could have done such a horrible thing? If, indeed, it had been murder. I tried to calm myself, to think sensibly. After all, Cousin Julia was hardly the most reputable source of information. Imagine the woman believing she could speak with the dead!

And this haunting she insisted upon — I was a person who prided herself on using reason. Certainly I did not believe in the existence of ghosts. The servants were probably imagining things.

I sighed. Given this old gloomy castle, a man found hanged by his own cravat — I shivered at the awful picture thus presented to me. No wonder the servants were seeing things.

Why had I let my desire for a child of my own override my usual good sense? Why had I contracted this loveless marriage and come to this godforsaken place?

I had no answers to my questions, of course. I threw myself into a chair in front of the fire and stared into the flames. There was little point in continuing to ask myself rhetorical questions. I *had* come to Grey Cliffs. I *had* married the earl. And now I could not in good conscience leave.

After all, three young lives depended on me. At least three.

My hands crept to my flat stomach, curling over it protectively. Should I even consider bringing a child into this place?

I sighed and swallowed over the lump in my throat. I wanted the child. I wanted it so badly that tears welled up in my eyes at the mere thought. But given my new husband's anger over that very desire, and the temper I had not known he possessed, could I expect, should I hope —

The door from the corridor creaked open. I hurried to my feet and turned, half expecting Ned with some new prank. But it was not Ned who stood there, it was my husband.

Edward smiled at me, but his eyes were clouded and dark. I suppressed a shudder. He seemed so different from the pleasant, reserved man I had married.

"I have come to take you for a walk," he said. "To show you your new home."

I kept my tongue between my teeth. He could at least have made it a request. But no. Not so much as a by-your-leave. Just a calm statement of fact. He was a man obviously used to giving orders — my new husband — and to having them obeyed.

Perhaps he detected my distemper from my expression. At any rate, his smile vanished. "Unless you have made other plans, of course."

I had no other plans. How should I? And such a walk would allow me to talk to him about the boy's dog. There was also Cousin Julia's disconcerting disclosure about the previous earl's death. But she must be mistaken about that. My husband would tell me she was mistaken and then I could forget the whole thing.

Edward mistook my thinking silence for a negative response and turned toward the door, presenting me with his broad back.

"Wait!" I cried. "I — I'll just get my cloak."

He turned back to me and I imagined I

saw a hint of pleasure in his brooding features. "Good," he said, and I heard the satisfaction in his voice. "I think you'll like the moor. It has its own wild beauty."

Some time later, I conceded that my husband was right. We had walked in silence for some minutes, through the twisted trees. Even though I knew the cause of their tortured look they still made me feel they were in agony. And finally we came out onto the rolling moor. The breeze was chill, but not extremely uncomfortable. I sniffed, noting it carried the smell of the sea.

The moor stretched out around us. Barren except for the wildness of sedge and gorse, there was still something exceptional about it. There was desolation of a sort, and yet the promise of a wild, savage beauty.

The earl moved closer to my side. "You should see it in the spring when the wildflowers bloom," he said. And then he chuckled. "You *will* see it in the spring when the wildflowers bloom."

I turned to look up into his face. His features had softened with his pleasure at this place. He looked younger, happier, and even more handsome.

He took another step toward me, his gaze traveling over my face. And then, quite sud-

73

denly, without a word of warning, he swept me into his arms.

They were strong arms, muscular, and they held me so close I smelled a hint of leather, a touch of spice. It was warm there, against his hard male body. I did not try to escape his grasp. My cloak had wrapped around me, making it difficult to move. And I felt a strangeness, held so close to this man I didn't know. But I did not really wish to move, because I felt something else, a ripple of what seemed like pleasure.

How could I take pleasure in being — I raised my head to look into his eyes, perhaps to — and knew I had made a mistake.

His eyes were dark — black as the rocks below my chamber window and just as hard. Yet they gleamed with something warm, something burning.

Then he bent his head and his lips covered mine. I shivered, but I was not cold. Indeed, a raging heat swept through my limbs, leaving me as weak and helpless as a child after a fever. But no child ever experienced the shocking emotions that invaded my body at the moment his tongue encountered mine.

I could not help myself, I cried out against his lips.

My husband raised his head, his eyes gone

even harder and now stone cold. His lips curled in what approached a sneer. "Beware, Hester, you will get no child if you refuse me."

I had been about to apologize, to explain — though not the precise nature of the feelings that even then made me blush — but his gruff tone and annoyed expression pinched my pride. So instead I simply replied, "I know, milord. I shall endeavor to do better."

Such a soft answer seemed to take him by surprise and for a moment his features warmed again. He reached out, pulling up my hood, which had fallen back during our embrace. "I'm sure you will," he said, touching my cheek with a warm finger. "I'll see to it."

The words were a threat, that much seemed plain. Yet they were spoken with so much tenderness, so much warmth, that I felt that awful heat rising in me again and could not reply.

He didn't seem to take this amiss, but removed his arm from around me, and twining the fingers of one hand through mine, turned back toward the moor. "Shall we walk a little farther? Tell me, now that you've met him, what do you think of Ned?"

That was the opening I sought and immediately I launched into a recital of our tour of the castle and his topics of discussion.

My husband laughed outright when he heard about the snake in the schoolroom desk. "Carolington was right," he said. "You can handle any young boy."

His eyes seemed to say something else, something more, but I nodded and hurried on. "I was a little concerned with this talk of priest holes — that could be dangerous."

Edward shrugged. "The boy has been warned. I think he will listen."

"I hope so." I hesitated, my gaze returning to the moor in front of us. I swallowed, trying to steady my voice. "Edward, Edward, I —"

He stopped short and turned toward me, his eyes boring into mine. "Hester, don't hesitate. If you've something to say to me, then out with it. Remember, I'm your husband."

"I know that," I said, pushing to the back of my mind the embarrassing knowledge that this man was my husband — so far at least — in name only. "Very well then." I took a deep breath. "It's about Ned's dog."

Edward's face softened. "Captain?"

"Yes. The boys tells me the dog is forbidden entry to the castle."

"Yes." It looked like Edward was about to smile.

"Something about a snake and the last governess," I went on.

Edward frowned. "The boy had to be reprimanded."

"Yes, of course," I said. "I am in perfect agreement about that. But —"

"Yes, Hester?" Edward raised an eyebrow. "Go on."

"I promised him I would speak to you about the dog, to see if he might be allowed back in the nursery."

"Is that what you would advise?"

He must know that. Otherwise why should I ask? He was playing some sort of game with me. I braced myself, waiting for his outburst of temper, and said, "Yes, I think —"

"Fine. I leave all such decisions up to you. Shall we walk on?"

I was stunned. Why had he conceded so easily? "Yes, I — Thank you."

"There's no need for thanks," he said as we resumed our walk and he took my hand in his again. "I married you to give Ned a mother. Why should I prevent you from acting as a mother would? Or *should?*"

The bitterness of his tone made me know he was thinking of *her*, the beautiful Royale who had run off, deserted her husband and her son. I glanced at Edward, observing how his jaw had tightened.

"Ned is quite an intelligent boy," I has-tened to remark. "I'm sure he will come to love me. And I him." I swallowed a lump in my throat, wishing I could erase the look of hurt I'd glimpsed in my husband's eyes.

The fingers that held mine tightened. "Yes," Edward said, his voice husky. "Ned will come to love you. I'm sure of it."

For one wild moment my heart pounded in my throat. For that moment I expected Edward to go on, to say that he, too, could grow to love me. But of course he said no such thing, believing that he might was all a figment of my imagination. I *wanted* him to love me. Why, I cannot say precisely except, perhaps, that I wished my child — our child — to grow up in a loving family.

But Edward said no more and I, swal-lowing my disappointment, tried to look around, to drink in the savage beauty of this wild place, a beauty I knew appealed to my husband.

But I could not forget Cousin Julia's sus-picions. They rankled in my mind like a thistle in a finger and I could not be content till I had answers. So I gathered my courage and spoke. "Edward?"

"Yes, Hester?"

He didn't stop walking and I was grateful.

I wasn't sure I wished to see his face when I asked the question that was searing through my mind.

"Edward, how did your father die?"

He scowled but did not stop or turn. "Why do you ask?"

"Because I want to know."

He stopped then and swung around to face me. The afternoon sun behind his back cast his face into obscurity so I could see nothing but a looming black shadow. My heart rose up in my throat and my knees took to trembling. I was alone on the moor with a man of great anger, great passion. I tasted primeval fear.

He grabbed me by the upper arm and shook me slightly. "Hester! I want an answer. Who's been talking to you!"

I saw I would have to tell him. I moistened my lips. "Cousin Julia told me about his death — the unusual mariner of it."

He laughed harshly, his hands dropping away from my arms. "You mean hanging himself by his own cravat?"

I nodded, swallowing my fear. "I — Why should a man do such a thing?" I asked, dismayed to hear the quiver in my voice.

Edward sighed. "I don't know. The physician said there was nothing wrong with him. No fatal illness or anything like that."

I tried to keep my voice steady. "Your mother? When did she die?"

"If you mean did he die because he had lost her, the answer is no. She died when I was quite young."

He sighed again. "One thing you must understand, Hester. My father was not a popular man. He was a hard man, always after more — more money, more power, more women."

He paused. "And he had made many enemies. Ask Uncle Phillip. He often bore the brunt of my father's anger. There was no one to say a good word for the old man. When he died, people began to whisper 'murder.' They even pointed the finger at me." He paused, frowning fiercely. "I suppose I was the logical choice, but I can assure you, I had nothing to do with my father's death."

He turned back to the moor, drawing me on. "It's entirely possible that he killed himself. In the last year before his death he had begun to act strangely. He'd always been a violent man, often in fits of rage breaking whatever was in reach. But then he became very quiet, watching people and saying nothing."

Edward shook his head. "It was like he'd become another person."

"You mean," I ventured, wondering at my own temerity, "that perhaps his mind was disturbed?"

His reply was curt. "Yes, perhaps."

He walked on in silence for some moments while I wrestled with this new and surprising knowledge.

First murder, now madness! Was every new day to bring me more dismaying information about this disquieting family?

I gulped. I had thought Cousin Julia and Uncle Phillip somewhat eccentric. But perhaps madness, true madness, ran in the family, was in the blood that ran through their veins!

I swallowed hastily. "Your mother — how did she die?"

"How?" Edward stopped again, but this time the sun was behind me and I saw his handsome features twisted into a frown. "From loneliness. From neglect. From lack of love."

The pain in his voice was so intense that for a moment I could not reply. Then I said, "But Edward, those things do not kill."

"You're quite right," he replied coldly. "*He* killed her."

My shock must have registered on my face for he laughed harshly. "No, not like *that*. Not with a weapon. She died trying to give him another son."

I experienced the strongest urge to take this big man into my arms and comfort him like I would have a hurt little boy. Of course I did not.

"You might as well know now," he went on brusquely. "Someone is sure to tell you soon. I despised my father. I hated him!"

I sucked in my breath. Could he have —

Almost as though I'd spoken my thoughts, he answered them. "But I didn't kill him. As God is my witness, I did not kill him!"

His eyes searched mine intently and I knew he wanted some response from me. It came from my heart. "I believe you," I said firmly. "I believe you."

Chapter Six

The rest of our walk was uneventful. By common consent we spoke only of the moor. Edward named for me the various grasses and plants, pointing out the sedge, the gorse, the samphire.

Duly I observed them and duly I admired the great stones that lay about, as though scattered by some giant hand. Edward spoke, too, of the people who had left those stones behind them, people of long ago, but I paid little real attention — my thoughts returning time and again to the puzzling matter of his father's death.

I spoke no more about it, however, and in due time we returned to the castle for dinner.

The day's conversation had left my nerves on edge and the approach of darkness — and bedtime — did nothing to calm them.

Cousin Julia and Uncle Phillip were both quite silent through the meal and then slipped away, leaving me alone with my husband.

"You look weary," Edward said. "Perhaps you should retire early."

I did not know how to respond to this. Nor did I care to admit to myself that I wished to retire with him. "I — I am not particularly tired," I said, but my voice lacked conviction and in truth I was weary.

"You look weary," he repeated, in a voice that brooked no resistance. "You'd best go up now."

At another time I might have argued with him. I certainly did not care to let him think he could order me about like a common servant. But I *was* weary. And there was a strange look about his eyes, a look that seemed almost tender.

I got to my feet. "Good night, then," I said, and despising myself for the tremor I heard in my voice, I turned toward the stairs.

"Good night, wife."

The strangest sensation quivered down my spine. I was Edward's wife in the eyes of the law. And I knew I would be his wife in more than that whenever he decided to make it so. The thought turned my knees weak and raised that heat in me again so that I could feel my very cheeks burning I picked up a candelabra and began to ascend the great stairs.

The hall was dark and gloomy, always pervaded by a chill that seeped into the bones. But that night I felt little of it. The fire that burned through my veins drove all else before it and heated my very flesh!

I reached my chamber and set the candelabra upon the bedside table. The maid Betty had been there before me, lighting candles, turning back the covers, laying out my nightdress.

I sighed as I looked at it. It was much patched and darned, poor thing, but then I had never expected anyone to see me in it — least of all a handsome husband. For a moment I gave myself up to wishing for some frivolous feminine adornments — ribbons and bows, pretty gowns. Perhaps then Edward would —

I pushed the thought from my mind and summoned Betty to help me undress. When she was gone, I sat before the mirror in my nightdress and brushed my hair the required one hundred strokes. I studied my reflection in the glass, wondering what my husband saw when he looked at me. Did he find me attractive? Did he *wish* to consummate our marriage? His kiss that afternoon had seemed to indicate so, yet he had sent me up to bed alone.

In exasperation, I threw down the hairbrush and got to my feet. I would go to bed, I told myself as I blew out the candles. And I would sleep.

Surprisingly enough, I did just that. I was indeed weary and had not been in bed long before I drifted off into slumber.

When I wakened, the room was quite dark. It took a moment for me to realize where I was. And then I heard the sound.

It was not an ordinary sound. There was something frightening, something sinister and unearthly about it.

"Go-o-o-o-o —" a voice breathed. "Leave — this — cursed — place."

I lay frozen in the great bed, staring into the Stygian darkness. But I could see nothing, nothing but the deep black of midnight. I swallowed. Was this the ghost Cousin Julia had talked about? But I did not believe in ghosts.

"Who — who are you?" I whispered, finally getting my tongue to work.

"Leave — this — place," the voice repeated in dire tones.

"I will do no such —" I began, and then I felt it. A hand! A chill ghostly hand touched my cheek. A scream forced its way out of my throat. It was followed by another.

I squeezed my eyes shut and tried to stop myself. But the feel of that cold, clammy hand lingered on my cheek. I simply had to scream — and go on screaming.

The heavy oak door crashed open, hitting the wall with a thud. "Hester!" Edward rushed across the room to the bed. "Hester! What's wrong?"

I opened my eyes to the welcome sight of my husband's face shining in the moonlight. Never had a human being looked so wonderful to me.

I threw myself, sobbing, into his arms. "He — he was here!"

Edward dropped down on the great bed and held me close against his chest, his warm strong chest. "Easy, Hester."

"Oh, it was horrible!"

"It's all right, my dear."

Gradually my sobs ceased and I lay trembling in my husband's arms. "There now," he said. "It will be all right." He smoothed the hair away from my forehead. "It was only a bad dream."

I tried to protest. "No, it was —"

"You must have fallen asleep and then you dreamed." He held me close, patting my back as I might pat a child.

"But —"

His face was so close to mine. The memory of that kiss on the moor twisted inside me and my body began to experience those sensations of heat. It was then I recalled that I was wearing only my nightdress and my husband was holding me in his arms.

"You're trembling like a leaf," he said tenderly. "Shall I stay with you?"

The warmth in his eyes, the touch of his fingers on my cheek, left little doubt as to what would transpire if he stayed. I looked up into his heated eyes. "Yes," I whispered. "Stay."

He smoothed my hair one more time. "Let me just light a candle," he said and rose to shut the door. "This place gets drafty."

I watched him cross the room, so strong, so handsome, and the trembling in my limbs had nothing to do with ghostly voices in the darkness. I was about to become a wife and I both feared and anticipated that event.

When he returned to the bed, Edward looked down at me from hooded eyes. "Shall I leave the candle burning?"

I hesitated. I was innocent of all knowledge of lovemaking and in my modesty would have preferred the darkness. But even Edward's presence could not completely dispel the memory of that clammy touch. "Yes, please," I whispered.

He began to undress and I tried to close

my eyes, but could not. He seemed so nonchalant, dropping his clothing piece by piece upon the floor, then turning to me with a smile. Of course I had seen male bodies, Jeremy's when he was little, but I had never seen a full-grown man without his clothes. Such a magnificent man. My breath caught in my throat.

He climbed into the great bed and pulled me into the crook of his arm, right against that warm male body. "Do you want to talk about your dream?" he asked, his lips against my cheek.

I knew that I should tell him I did not believe it had been a dream. But he was so close, the heat of his body burning through my nightdress inflamed my very skin.

"Sweet Hester," he whispered. "Beautiful Hester."

That heat that glowed inside me burned ever brighter, and when he pulled me closer and covered my lips with his, I lost all thought of anything but the man who held me.

Sometime later, I lay nestled in the crook of his arm, my nightdress discarded on the floor. He kissed the tip of my ear. "You will have your child, Hester." He chuckled. "And soon, I think. Very soon."

I sighed and moved closer to his warmth. No one had ever told me what I might expect in the marriage bed, so I had brought with me no expectations. But even if someone *had* told me, I would not have believed them. Such pleasure seemed almost impossible.

Edward's lips moved across my cheek to my throat. "Is it —" I turned toward him. "Is it always like this?"

He laughed, catching my bottom lip between his teeth in a way that set my body on fire again and made it move against his. "Yes," he murmured against my mouth. "It will always be this good."

We slept finally, our limbs entwined, and with his strong body enfolding mine I felt no fear. The morning sun, shining in my eyes, woke me. The room was cold, the candle burned down. My nightdress lay still upon the floor, but I had no need of it. Under the comforter I was cozy and warm. My husband lay, one arm across my breasts, one leg over mine. He stirred, and to my dismay I felt my desire rising. The heat flooded my cheeks at the thought of the night before, of what we had done. Edward must think me so wanton.

"Good morning," he said, his dark face so close to mine.

"Good morning," I murmured.

His lips grazed my cheek and my traitorous body moved. My husband laughed. "Lovely Hester," he whispered, drawing me once more into a passionate embrace. "Hungry Hester."

Sometime later, he left my bed. Striding in naked splendor to the door that opened into his room, he blew me a kiss. "Stay cozy till I send Betty to help you dress."

As he shut the door to his room, I sighed luxuriantly and stretched, letting my hands stray toward my stomach. *Now* I was a wife and perhaps already I was on my way to becoming a mother.

Betty came in good time and helped me into my gown, clicking her tongue as she retrieved Edward's discarded clothing. "Just like a little one a man be," she chuckled. "When he be wanting *that*." She looked at me slyly, perhaps wondering if I would take offense, but on that morning nothing could have offended me. I simply laughed with her.

"I will see you later, Betty," I said when I was dressed. "I will be taking over some of the boys' care." I paused. "But I wonder, would you continue to look out for them?"

"Of course, milady." She eyed me leerily. "But them twins —"

"It's not uncommon for twins to create their own language," I said calmly.

Betty's eyes widened. "You mean that ain't the devil atalking through them?"

"Of course not, Betty. It's just a language they've made up."

Betty grinned. "Well I never! Them little rascals! Sure, milady, I'll be watching of 'em."

I hummed under my breath as I descended the great stairs. The hall was just as gloomy as ever, but my spirits were so high that even the darkness seemed warm.

The sideboard was loaded with food. I filled a plate, eager to eat and get to the boys. I planned to start that day with history, teaching them more about the reign of Henry VIII. They should know more about that monarch than his abhorrence of things Catholic.

I had put away a good amount of food and was feeling quite pleased with myself and with life in general when I heard a whistling in the hall.

I looked up in time to see a man enter the room. I knew at once that he was Edward's brother, Robert. The family resemblance was there, though Robert did not appear to be nearly as handsome as my husband.

He was younger, but there was a certain slackness around his overfull lips, a certain puffiness around his jaded eyes, that bespoke a life of dissipation.

The glance he threw my way on first entering the room soon became a detailed perusal of my person. "Well, well," he exclaimed. "Edward didn't say you were such a beauty."

He crossed and took my hand, raising it to his lips in a practiced gesture, but I remained unimpressed. Rakes had always seemed to me at best rather useless creatures.

"No words of welcome from such a vision of loveliness?" He grinned at me and I conceded that he had a certain charm. "Has she perhaps the voice of a frog?"

"Her voice is quite normal." Edward came into the room, moving directly to my side.

I had already removed my fingers from his brother's grasp. Edward took them possessively in his own. A surge of warmth rippled through me.

"Have you seen your sons yet?" I asked Robert.

He shrugged. "No. They're well enough, though, I suppose."

I glared at the man. "Well enough! And

how would you know? Man, these are your children, your own flesh and blood! Have you no feeling for them?"

He didn't seem the least perturbed. "My dear Hester, you will get nowhere by yelling at me in that shrewish fashion. As Edward will be only too glad to tell you."

My husband's tightened lips confirmed this and he nodded grimly.

Robert laughed. "It's no use, Hester. I cannot be reformed. I'm too much like our dear departed father for reformation. Give me wine, women, and song — and I'm happy."

"You're disgusting," Edward said grimly. "How long do you plan to stay this time?"

"Till quarter day, of course." He cast a shrewd glance at Edward. "Unless, of course, you'll give me my money now."

Edward cursed, then looked to me and clamped his mouth shut.

"Forgive my dear brother," Robert said with false cheerfulness. "He's forgotten how to act around a woman."

This I knew to be a lie, but I did not respond to his baiting.

"The care of the earldom weighs heavy on his shoulders," Robert continued. "So heavy." And he sent Edward a provoking look.

I sighed. It was easy to see that there was no love lost between the brothers. But I could hardly blame Edward for that. After the scandal he had suffered with his wife, he must be doubly wounded by his brother's indiscretions. And for the man to behave so callously toward his own children —

I turned to my husband and smiled. He finally was my husband, and much to my satisfaction. He smiled back at me, warmly, tenderly.

Robert snorted. "Perhaps I should leave you lovebirds to your billing and cooing."

Edward's expression hardened. "That won't be necessary. Besides, I wish to have some words with you in private."

"Of course, brother dear."

I did not see how Robert could be so nonchalant. If Edward were glaring at me in that grim fashion, I knew I should be really alarmed.

But Edward was smiling at me. "I'll see you later, dear," he said, and bent to put a kiss on my brow. Then he straightened. "Come, Robert, let's go to the drawing room."

Chapter Seven

After my husband and his brother disappeared down the hall, I finished my tea and set out for the nursery. I had settled on a plan of attack — sometimes winning over a boy seemed rather like fighting a war. But the results were usually much better.

I pushed open the nursery door. The twins were at play upon the hearth, their lead soldiers battling with miniature troops of Napoleon.

Ned, however, stood across the room, gazing out the narrow window toward the stables.

"Good morning," I said, putting as much cheerfulness as I could into my voice.

"Morning, milady." Betty raised her head from her mending and nodded.

The twins looked up and smiled. "Good," said one. "Morning," said the other.

I returned their smiles. They seemed quite healthy in their outlook — Robert's children — perhaps it was just as well he had not spent much time with them. Such a man could be a bad influence.

Ned turned from the window, his eyes

eager. "Did you —" He stopped himself. "Good morning, Hester."

"Good morning, Ned."

I saw the boy's mouth quiver slightly. He was anxious to know about the dog but obviously afraid to ask.

"Well," I said, smiling at them all. "I have a piece of good news."

Ned's face lit up, but he said nothing more.

"Ned, your father says you may bring Captain back to the nursery."

"Capital!" the twins cried in unison.

"He's mine!" Ned said fiercely, scowling at the twins. "All mine."

The twins exchanged a look, but kept silent.

"Of course the dog is yours," I agreed. "And you will want to bring him in soon, but perhaps you should wait till we've had our lessons."

The boy's face fell. "Of course," he said slowly, reluctantly. "Captain likes it outside."

"On the other hand," I went on, as though considering all the possibilities, "it might be useful to have him along with us."

All three of them stared at me, but it was Ned who echoed, "Along with us?"

"Yes," I said. "I thought we'd have our

history lesson while we look for secret passageways and the priest hole you told me about."

The three of them gaped at me. Finally Ned asked, "You mean we're going to *look* for them? Really *look* for them?"

"Yes," I said. "It should be an interesting lesson. Of course we could stay in the classroom and just —"

The twins got to their feet, their make-believe battles forgotten. "Dogs're good." "At smelling things out," they observed in tandem.

"Maybe he can find something," Ned said, for once not disagreeing with the others.

I had no idea what the dog might find, but Ned was obviously eager to get the animal back into the castle. "Yes," he said, nodding. "He's good at sniffing things out. I'm sure he can help. I'll go get him."

He was halfway to the door before he stopped. "Can I?" he turned to ask, his eyes pleading.

"Yes, Ned. But come right back. We'll be ready."

When Ned returned short minutes later, the dog was at his heels — a nondescript black dog, stocky, medium-sized, greying at the muzzle. He took one look at me and started yipping. Ned quieted him. "It's all right, Captain. Hester belongs here."

I swallowed hastily over the lump that had risen in my throat. That was good! The boy was already on his way to accepting me.

The dog came to me then, sniffing my skirts. I knelt and looked into his deep brown eyes. "Hello, Captain," I said softly, stretching out a tentative hand. The dog sniffed it too, finally gave it a lick, and turned back to the boy.

"He likes you," Ned said, his hand resting possessively on the dog's head. "He only licks people he likes."

"That's right," said the twins.

Hiding my satisfaction, I got to my feet. "Now, where shall we start?"

An hour later we were back in the nursery. We had found no secret passageways, no priest hole, but what we had found was more important — a common ground where we could meet and get to know each other.

Certainly Ned and the twins were still not friends, but at least they were able to speak to each other with some civility.

We gathered around the table then and Ned read to me. When I told him to pass the book to Peter, the boy shook his head. "Can't," he said.

"Now, Peter, come. Give it a try."

Peter and Paul exchanged some unintelligible words then Peter turned to me. "Can't neither of us read nor write."

"Oh." How stupid of me to have forgotten the twins' origin. "Well," I said, "we'll fix that."

Paul stared at me. "Don't need to read. Gonna work the fields."

"Of course you need to read," I said firmly.

Peter raised an eyebrow, blue eyes very like his father's boring into mine. "Why?"

Why indeed? I thought. Given Robert's attitude they were lucky to have a roof over their heads, food to eat, and clothes to wear. An education was quite a luxury.

Still I persisted. These children were in my charge and while I was responsible for them, they would learn. "Because reading and writing will help you —"

"Don't see how," Peter interrupted.

I hesitated, trying to think of some good reply. But while I sought in my mind for some acceptable reason they would understand, the door opened.

"Hello," Robert said, giving me a practiced smile. "The chatelaine at work. You make a pretty picture."

I stiffened, his compliment making me

uneasy. I disliked his rakish attitude and I meant to stand for none of that behavior in front of the children.

When he got no response from me, Robert turned to Ned. "What are you studying today?"

The boy smiled. "This morning we looked for secret passageways. Hester got Father to let Captain back into the nursery. And now we're reading." Ned looked at the twins. "Only they can't."

Robert frowned. "Can't read, is it? As I remember it's rather a tough job at first." He crossed the room to lean over, his face close to mine. "What seems to be the problem?"

"There is no problem," I replied, leaning in the other direction, away from him. Why must the man get so close to me? "The twins have had no lessons, so naturally they can't read."

"They said they won't need it," Ned volunteered. "Wish I didn't have to learn."

Robert frowned. "Of course you have to learn. You're a gentleman's son."

I couldn't believe the man's calloused disregard for his own children. The poor things had already suffered enough, probably been called all kinds of ugly names by the village children. And now — now their father was ignoring them, acting like they were invisible. And to add insult to injury, he was making up to Ned.

"Reading and writing are useful accomplishments for any person," I said firmly. "They will be useful to the twins."

For the first time, Robert turned his attention to his sons. The twins stared back at him, their expressions wary. When they exchanged remarks in their private language, I could not understand the sense of them, but I knew by the inflection that one questioned the other. Were they discussing their father?

"So, Peter, Paul," Robert said, his eyes narrowing. "Do you know who I am?"

Paul's face grew guarded. "You're Ned's Uncle Robert."

Robert nodded, but he looked almost disappointed. "What else do you know about me?"

Paul opened his mouth, then closed it again. "Not allowed to say," Peter observed.

I almost gasped. These children had been forbidden to name their own father. "Why?" I asked.

"Made Gramps mad," Peter said, sending his father a sly look.

Robert nodded. "I see."

I swallowed a curse. Was the man so

hard-hearted he couldn't acknowledge his own children?

"Gramps isn't here," I pointed out. "So it's all right to say."

Peter and Paul exchanged another string of unintelligible syllables. "You're right," Paul said to me. He turned to Peter.

"We know," Peter said. "You're our father."

Somewhat to my surprise, Robert smiled. "Right," he said. "And now that you're living in the castle, you'll need to learn to read and write. Will you do that for me? Will you learn?"

I gaped like any country bumpkin. The unmitigated gall of the man — to ignore his sons for six years and then expect them to obey him!

But Peter and Paul didn't hesitate, they didn't consult in their private language, they didn't even look at each other. "Yes," they said together. "We will."

And while Ned and I watched in surprise, Robert took his sons by the hands and went to look at their tin soldiers, lying still upon the hearth.

The rest of the day went quite well. After Robert left the nursery, with promises to his sons to spend more time with them, we went on to lessons in addition.

By the time we finished it was almost the hour for lunch. I decided to leave the boys to their meal with Betty and started for the door.

"Hester?" It was Ned, his voice hesitant.

I turned. "Yes?"

"When are you coming back?"

I hid my smile. "I think for a while we'll have lessons in the morning. In the afternoons you boys may play."

Ned's face lit up. "Or ride?"

I swallowed my sudden fear. "Yes. Your father told me that you have a pony."

Ned nodded.

"What about Peter and Paul?"

Ned frowned, but it looked somewhat put on to me. "I don't know. They weren't here when Father bought my pony."

I turned to the twins. "Do you ride?"

" 'Course." "We do."

"Then I shall send word to the stables. The three of you may ride together."

Ned looked somewhat put out. "Unless," I added, "you would prefer to stay in and have more lessons."

The twins sent Ned a disgusted look. "No, no," he hurried to say. "That last governess used to tell me that fresh air was good for me."

I swallowed my smile. "Very well. You may ride this afternoon."

After I freshened up, I went down the dark stairs to the dining room. The hall was still chill and dank, but I was warmed by thoughts of seeing Edward. My truant thoughts actually strayed to the coming evening — and bedtime.

I flushed and hurried on. Perhaps eventually I would get used to being Edward's wife, to feeling his kisses and —

I forced myself to push such disturbing thoughts from my mind. Darkness would come — and with it the closeness I longed for. In the meantime, I entered the empty dining room and filled my plate.

My appetite had always been healthy and my morning's work had made me hungry. I was about half finished when Edward came in. I smiled at him — my husband — such a fine-looking man. "I was hoping to see you," I said.

He didn't return my smile. In fact, he frowned. He didn't fill a plate either, but advanced to the table and stood glaring down at me. "I have been wanting to speak to *you*," he said darkly.

My heart rose up in my throat. What had caused this sudden change in his behavior?

Only this morning he had folded me in passionate embraces. And now he was glaring at me as though I had become the worst kind of criminal. I couldn't help wondering how I had offended him, but a moment's recollection gave me no clue.

So I asked. "Edward, what is wrong? Why do you glare at me so?"

He scowled, his dark brows meeting in a fierce line. "Didn't I tell you?"

I got to my feet — it seemed easier to face him that way. I felt less frightened. "Tell me what?"

"What do you think you're doing?"

Now I was getting angry, fast losing patience at this foolish sort of interrogation. "Doing about what?" I demanded crossly. "For heaven's sake, Edward, make some sense! Whatever are you talking about?"

"Priest holes and secret passageways," he intoned darkly.

I still did not understand. "What about them?"

He stiffened and seemed to loom even larger. "You are encouraging the boys to look for them. This can only cause trouble."

The trouble was coming from Robert — I strongly suspected. Who else would have reported our excursion? "Edward," I kept my tone calm. "You know the boys are going to look for these anyway. Wouldn't it be wiser to have a grown-up along?"

He drew himself up even more — a big man, and in his present mood very threatening. "The boys are forbidden to look for secret passageways!" he thundered. "They are not to have their heads filled with talk of such things — secret chambers and priest holes, indeed! Have you no idea how dangerous this can be?"

My patience was exhausted. "Of course I know. That's why I thought it better for me to be along when they found them."

"It is *not* better," he cried. "You are *not* to look for such things, not to talk of such things. Is that understood?"

I drew myself up to my full height and met the blazing anger of his eyes. "Yes, milord," I said sharply. I was quite capable of anger myself. "You have made yourself amply clear."

He stared at me for a moment, then spun on his heel and stalked out.

I dropped into my chair again and continued my meal. I must eat, I reminded myself when I found the food had lost its flavor. If the new little life had started inside me, it must be nourished.

As I methodically chewed and swallowed, I considered my husband's rude behavior.

That he had a temper, I had known. But to be the object of it — and for such a patently ridiculous reason . . . No person living could keep boys that age from looking for an exciting secret passageway. Surely Edward must know that. He had been a boy himself.

I sighed and poured myself another cup of tea. How could the man who had loved me so passionately, held me so tenderly, now treat me like the meanest inferior! It was difficult to believe.

Yet, while my body was still warmed by the memory of his touch, my ears rang with the force of his angry pronouncement.

I would obey him. He was the earl and my husband. Obedience was his due. Still, I knew that obedience in this matter would serve no purpose. The boys would continue to search. They were, after all, boys.

Chapter Eight

The rest of the day passed uneventfully. I spent the afternoon familiarizing myself with the castle, getting to know the servants. I had a long, rather detailed discussion with the cook and was confident that our meals would show improvement.

And through it all, I puzzled over my husband's strange behavior. To show so much anger over a simple story of secret passageways. Why? Why had Edward been so upset?

I dressed for dinner, putting on my blue gown. But in the dining room I found only Uncle Phillip and Cousin Julia. Uncle Phillip was his usual baggy, mismatched self, liberally covered with dust and dried mud. I was getting used to his ragtag appearance.

But Cousin Julia was wearing a gown of cerise satin that contrasted sharply with her hair, which though she had liberally powdered it, was still a startling orange hue.

"Edward won't be here," Cousin Julia said, drawing her chair up to the table.

"How do you know?"

Cousin Julia tittered. "The spirits told me."

A chill crept down my spine. "Perhaps he's just a trifle late."

Cousin Julia shook her head. "No. He's been really detained."

Another frisson of fear slithered down my backbone. "I don't see how you can know such things. You must be guessing."

Uncle Phillip laughed, the deep booming laugh that seemed so strange coming from such a small man. "She doesn't need to guess," he explained. "She heard Edward tell Hillyer he was going out and wouldn't be back till bedtime."

A wave of disappointment rolled over me. I missed Edward. If he didn't come home till late . . . If he were still angry with me then . . .

I turned to Hillyer, now standing coldly by the door. "Did the earl give you such information?"

Hillyer inclined his head. "Yes, milady."

"Why didn't you tell me?"

Hillyer looked pained. "Begging your pardon, milady, but the earl didn't tell me to tell you." He straightened. "You see, when he goes out he always tells me where he's going and when he'll be back."

"Quite a commendable practice," I observed, "especially when he had no lady." I fixed the butler with a cold eye. "Now, of

110

course, I am here. And if the earl is called away, you'll be sure to inform me."

Hillyer shifted slightly, but his dour expression didn't change. "Yes, milady, I understand."

Uncle Phillip chuckled. "That's the way, m'girl. Show 'em who's in charge. It's important to be the one who *gives* orders."

Since Hillyer was still in the room, I found it a little difficult to reply, but Cousin Julia had no such qualms. "Got to watch the servants," she said. "Got to keep them in line."

"I'm sure Hillyer does an admirable job," I went on. "He was merely following his instructions."

Oh yes, I stuck up for the butler. It was my husband I wanted to berate. How could the man just walk out without a word to me? Was that the kind of life I had to look forward to?

"Tonight," Cousin Julia said.

I raised an eyebrow. It was obvious I had missed part of her pronouncement. She gave me a pained look. "The spirits are here tonight."

Uncle Phillip snorted. "Ridiculous! Poppycock! My brother would have laughed himself to death just listening to you."

Cousin Julia's beady little eyes gleamed.

She licked her lips. "Never you mind," she said. "My spirits are real. They come right into this castle. They talk to me."

Uncle Phillip made a face and winked at me, but I didn't respond. In my present mood I wished only to be alone. Still, these two misfits would be at each other's throats if I left the table early. And they did offer distraction of a sort.

"How do you know they are present?" I inquired. I would listen to anything to keep my mind off worrying over Edward.

Cousin Julia smiled mysteriously. "I *feel* them," she said. "Right here." And she put a pudgy finger in the middle of her forehead.

I thought that rather a strange place for a spirit to perch, but I refrained from saying so.

"Sometimes," Cousin Julia continued. "They move things."

"It's all a trick," Uncle Phillip pronounced. "Not that I don't believe in spirits." He leered. "But they're too busy to be talking to the likes of *her*."

Cousin Julia bristled, but said nothing. Obviously this was a running battle between the two.

"Now," Uncle Phillip said, "conjuring up Old Nick, that takes a real man." He straightened his bony shoulders. "And you've got to know how to do it." He turned to me eagerly. "You want me to show you?"

"Not tonight, Uncle Phillip." I pressed a hand to my forehead. "I seem to be getting the headache. I think I shall have to go up early." And I left the two of them, glaring at each other over Cook's rich dessert.

But I soon discovered that going to my room brought me no peace of mind. The huge bed, with its covers neatly pulled back and my nightdress spread upon it, seemed to mock me. Only that morning I had been so happy there. And now — my husband had stormed out without so much as a good-bye.

I sighed. This marriage had certainly not turned out as I'd expected. I'd looked for a recalcitrant child, yes. But murder and madness — that was too much.

I crossed the room to peer out at the ocean. Darkness had fallen some time past, but the clouds were not hiding the moon and its light danced on the waves washing the rocks below. I shivered. It was a long fall to those rocks — long and deadly.

A rap sounded on the door to the hall. I whirled. Edward! "Come in."

But it was not Edward, but Betty. She

came in and dropped me a curtsey. "The boys is all abed, milady. The scamps was that tired from their ride." She cast me a shy glance. "If I might be saying it, milady, things is different, you being here. Even fer such a short time. Them boys, I mean, they ain't squabbling like they was." She smiled, then blushed. "I know it ain't for a maid to be saying, but it's glad I am you've come."

"Thank you, Betty." I appreciated her kind words, especially as they were the only kind ones I had heard.

"And, milady, Mr. Phillip sent me." Betty's eyes grew wide. "He said as how he's fixing to call up old Lucifer. And maybe you'd like to see."

I shivered. I didn't believe Uncle Phillip could conjure up the devil, but I certainly had no desire to witness such an attempt, whether it failed or not.

"Not tonight, Betty. Tell him not tonight."

After Betty had helped me into my night-dress and left, I brushed my hair and climbed into the big bed. I did not, how-ever, blow out all the candles. Still, the room was dim and gloomy, and shadows lurked in every corner. Could there really be ghosts? Could the spirits of the dead really return?

It seemed most unlikely to me, practical and sensible as I was. But the gloominess of the room, and my being alone, and my worry over Edward's strange behavior all combined to leave me shivering under the covers.

I had always been a person who saw problems as challenges. I was sure the recalcitrant boys I dealt with could each be won over — all I needed was to find the right approach.

But now I was faced with a different sort of problem. How could I fight a ghost? How could I discover the real truth about the death of the previous earl? And how could I understand the dark moody man who was my husband?

I had no answers to any of my questions. But there was one thing I was sure of. I could not leave this place. I meant to be aunt to the twins. I had given my solemn word to be mother to Ned. These were heavy chains, binding me to Grey Cliffs. But the strongest, the person who held me there by the strongest chain, was the angry brooding man I had married.

I shivered there in the gloom for some time and then I did what I usually do when I can see no practical answer to my problems — I prayed.

And as always my prayers brought a

feeling of relief — and soon I dozed off.

I don't know whether a noise awoke me — or whether it was the sense of someone in the room with me. But I woke — quickly — with that startling heart-pounding fear, that cold sweat, that comes with a nightmare.

I must have uttered a cry of some kind when I saw the room was dark, for then I felt a hand touch my cheek. Even as I screamed I knew it was Edward's hand.

He gathered me against his warm chest. "Hester. Hester," he crooned. "It's all right. I'm here."

My trembling ceased and I felt safe. Whatever the reason for Edward's anger, that anger was gone. All I felt in his touch was affection.

"Hester, my dear Hester," he whispered. "Forgive my harshness earlier today."

A great welling of feeling choked me, making it impossible for me to speak. I swallowed hard.

His fingers caressed my cheek, moved slowly down my throat. "Hester, lovely Hester," he whispered against my ear. "Say you forgive me."

"I —" I struggled to maintain some semblance of sense. I couldn't let him think that he had only to touch me to elicit my forgiveness. I tried to hold myself stiff, though my

116

traitorous body wanted to melt into his. "Why?"

His lips grazed my ear. "Why should you forgive me?" he whispered, his voice husky.

"No, no. Why were you so angry?"

He settled me comfortably against his chest. He was so warm, so solid. I waited.

"Fear," he said finally. "I was afraid."

It seemed incongruous, this big strong man being afraid. "Afraid of what?" I asked, though I thought perhaps I knew.

"I have only just found you," he whispered, his voice muffled in my hair. "And the thought of losing you —" He clasped me tightly to him.

My heart pounded and a great wave of joy surged through me. It was *me* he was concerned about. I felt such an overwhelming happiness that it frightened me. And in that moment I saw the truth. I loved Edward so much that even if there had been no Ned, no twins, no unborn child to hold me to Grey Cliffs Castle, I would never think of leaving my husband.

He had not said he loved me, not in so many words, but his voice told me, his kisses, his touch. He bent to my mouth again. "My Hester," he whispered and I raised my lips to his, waiting for my husband to kiss me, to love me.

The next morning Edward left me early. With a kiss and a smile, he was off to attend to estate business. I rose and dressed, a very happy woman.

Our morning in the classroom was uneventful, but after lunch, remembering something I'd forgotten to tell the twins about the next day's lesson, I went in search of them.

In the nursery Betty sat by the fire, her needle ever busy with the mending. "Where are the boys?" I asked. "Did they go riding again?"

Betty shook her head. "Ned did. But one of them twins — I can't never tell them two apart — was whispering to the other. Something about pents and grams." Betty shrugged apologetically. "Didn't make no sense to me, milady."

Pents. Grams. What could the twins be talking about? And then I thought perhaps I knew. "Betty, did Uncle Phillip stop by the nursery today?"

Betty nodded. "He did, indeed, milady. Right after you left."

On no! Pentagrams! Uncle Phillip couldn't be — I rushed out.

Uncle Phillip's door stood ajar. I paused outside it, quieting myself. First, it was impossible to conjure up the devil. I firmly believed it impossible. And everyone knew the devil was to be summoned at midnight, at the witching hour, not in the middle of the day.

I took a deep breath and slowly pushed open the door. The sight that met my eyes made the hair stand up on my flesh!

In the center of the room, a room even gloomier than most in this dismal place, stood Uncle Phillip, his clothes dusty and mud-spattered. The rug had been rolled back, exposing the cold stone floor. And on that floor, laid out in white lines, was a great pentagram. Uncle Phillip stood in its center, eyes squeezed shut, chanting some unintelligible phrases.

That sight was frightening enough, but there was more. Beyond the pentagram the twins hovered. Their eyes tightly closed, their hands clasped, they were repeating Uncle Phillip's mad chant.

My fear gave way to anger. How dare the man involve innocent children in his nefarious schemes.

"Stop!" I shouted, my voice hoarse with rage.

Uncle Phillip's face turned ashen. His eyes flew open and he stared at me as though he expected to see Lucifer himself!

Then his expression changed. Relief swept over his features and his color slowly returned to normal.

"H-Hester! What are you doing here?"

"I'm looking for the twins," I said, glancing at the culprits who now stood grinning at me. I gave Uncle Phillip a hard look. "How can you do such things in front of the boys?"

He shrugged. "They wanted to watch."

"Well, they can't. I forbid it! Peter, Paul, come along now."

I used my sternest voice and the twins did not protest. They crossed the room, carefully skirting the pentagram, and reached my side.

With a last look at Uncle Phillip, I marched them out and down the hall. "Did you see his face?" Peter asked his brother.

Paul giggled. "For a minute there he thought he'd done it, really got the old devil to come."

I was convinced the twins were right. Certainly my appearance had startled Uncle Phillip almost as much as the devil's would have. But I didn't let on that I heard them.

When we reached the nursery, I put on my severest face. "Now," I said, facing the boys. "There will be no more of this. No more! Do you understand?"

The twins nodded.

"Why aren't you out riding?"

There was a moment's silence, then Paul said, "Ned wanted to go alone."

Peter nodded. "Anyhow, he rides too fast. Our horses can't keep up."

I nodded. "Well, then stay in, but keep away from Uncle Phillip."

They nodded, their eyes clear and innocent. "Yes, Hester. We will."

Had I known them better, I would have found such docility suspect. But I thought them suitably reprimanded and turned my thoughts elsewhere. As I left the nursery, I heard them exchange a comment in their private language, but I gave it no thought. And for that I would later have cause for regret.

Chapter Nine

That afternoon I spent exploring the castle on my own. In spite of Edward's fears for my safety, I thought it far more sensible to find the priest hole and the secret passageways. If their location were known, there would be no danger of anyone being trapped there until their bones were — as Ned had so dramatically put it — nothing but dust.

But my explorations turned up nothing and I returned to my room to dress for dinner. My blue gown was beginning to show the effects of wear and I was glad I had taken Edward at his word and sent to the village for the dressmaker. My governess clothes had been plain and serviceable — and much limited in number — so that I found dressing meant wearing the same few gowns. But soon my new ones would arrive.

I finished dressing, gave a pat to my hair, and hurried down to dinner. Uncle Phillip was there before me, in another of his collection of mismatched clothes and his sloppy carpet slippers. He gave me a look half-sheepish, half-pleading, and I knew he didn't want me to tell Edward that I'd caught him trying to summon Lucifer while the twins looked on. But I had made no such promise and was not yet sure what I would do.

This evening Cousin Julia's gown was of a subdued shade of rose, actually rather pretty, but her orange hair contrasted with it so that the effect was still unfortunate. She greeted me with a strange, sly smile. "No need to worry," she said. "He'll be here tonight."

I supposed she meant Edward. "I know," I replied, trying not to sound smug, trying not to look like the satisfied wife I felt. I was about to make some dull remark about the weather when Robert came in.

Cousin Julia took a look at his fashionable attire and tittered. "Going out tonight?" she asked with a knowing smile.

Robert shrugged. "A man has to have some diversion."

Uncle Phillip snorted. "So that's what they call it nowadays."

Smiling, Robert turned to me. At another time, under other conditions, perhaps I would have felt flattered, but at that time I only felt uneasy. I loved my husband — loved him deeply and with a passion I hadn't suspected I possessed — and to have another man, especially his brother, fawn over me, made me most uneasy.

However, Robert did not seem to perceive my distress and raised my hand to his lips. I barely kept myself from jerking it away. Was it Robert's touch that was distasteful? Or was it that now my flesh only wished for my husband's gentle caress?

I withdrew my fingers as soon as I decently could. "Good evening, Robert," I said. "How are you this evening?"

"Looking at a lovely lady always makes me delighted," he replied, with a false smile that reminded me of a naughty boy trying to smile his way out of some mischief.

I felt harsh words rising to my lips, but I bit them back. I was new here. It was not up to me to criticize Edward's brother.

Then my heart leaped. Edward, *my* Edward, had appeared in the doorway. He looked so strong, so handsome. My heart sang and my body began to flush with warmth.

"Good evening," he said, his gaze meeting mine, his voice husky. He crossed the room to stand by my side. His presence there made me feel happy, safe.

"Good evening, Edward." I hoped my voice didn't give me away. I didn't understand how it could have happened so quickly, but I knew that it had. I was besotted with my husband.

Robert gave me a startled glance and I perceived that I had not succeeded in hiding my secret. But I did not care. I loved my husband. And he loved me. Soon he would tell me so.

Uncle Phillip made an indelicate sound, glanced quickly at me, and smiled sheepishly. Cousin Julia tittered. "So you're going to dine with us tonight, Edward."

Edward gave her a dry look. "I believe that is my custom."

Robert smirked at me. "My dear brother *believes* in custom," he said. "As you'll soon discover."

To my surprise Edward's face began to turn crimson. He appeared to struggle with his feelings for a moment, then he burst forth with, "That will be enough! Quite enough!"

But Robert would not be quieted. "Just a quirk of fate," he said with a sneer, "that's all that kept me from being the earl. You were born first, that's all." He smiled and a shiver slithered down my backbone. "Another quirk is all it would take, a little accident, of one sort or another — and the earldom would be mine."

I gasped at such terrible effrontery, but no one even noticed. They were all staring at Robert.

Finally Cousin Julia tittered again, breaking the tension that hung so heavily in the room. "Don't mind him," she said with a knowing glance at me. "Robert's just mad 'cause he can't get his money till quarter day."

"I *could*." Robert glared at his brother. "But Edward refuses to give it to me."

Edward's face was still crimson, his jaw grimly taut. I reached out to touch his sleeve. His expression didn't lighten but when his gaze met mine, he swallowed several times and then said in a voice whose calmness belied the grimness of his face, "The terms of Robert's allowance are not mine. They are my father's terms. He made his wishes known — and I abide by them."

"Of course you do," Robert said. "Because you're a stickler after propriety."

Under the circumstances, I thought that barb extremely unfair. Robert must know what Edward's wife had done to him. How could he treat his brother so cruelly, how could he remind him of that disgraceful episode?

"You are right," Edward replied caustically. "I am. Of course, propriety has never been of much concern to you, so I suppose I cannot expect you to think of it. But I warn you."

He turned the full force of his frown on his brother. To his credit, Robert did not cringe. For a moment I wondered how I would have reacted had Edward turned such a scornful look on me. I decided I wished never to find out.

"I warn you," Edward repeated. "There will be no more scandal around our name in this village. If you cause any scandal, any talk, you will find that even quarter day does not arrive for you."

Robert stiffened. "You wouldn't! You can't!"

Edward shrugged. "I would. And I can. And you had best believe me."

"Oh, I believe you." Robert scowled. "And now, if you're through with your pious pronouncements, I'll be off to search for better company."

Edward did not rise to this bait. He seemed to have taken his temper in hand. "As you wish. Only remember what I have told you."

Robert shot his cuffs and ostentatiously admired the lace that edged them. Then he gave me that lazy, rakish grin and sauntered out without another word.

I looked at Edward. I was worried about my husband. Such anger couldn't be good for him. And with the taint of madness hanging over the family . . . I tried to push such thoughts from my mind. Edward was a good man. He loved his son. He let his brother's bastards live in the castle. He was gentle to me.

I took my husband's hand. "Come," I said. "Let's have our dinner."

But our dinner was not to be peaceful. We were barely into the first course when Cousin Julia looked up from her mountainously full plate and said, "I think Friday will be a good night."

"A good night for what?" I inquired.

"For our séance."

My fork almost fell from my suddenly numb fingers. "Séance?" I repeated, staring at her.

"Yes. Haven't you someone you wish to communicate with?"

My thoughts flew to Jeremy, my dear departed Jeremy. Though I knew such a wish was futile, how I wanted to speak to him. "No," I said. "No one." But I heard the longing in my voice.

Cousin Julia looked at me, her eyes wide. "There must be *someone.*"

Edward looked up from his plate. "Cousin Julia," he said sharply. "That will be enough. If Hester says there is no one she wishes to speak to, then there is no one."

Cousin Julia nodded, but her beady little eyes gleamed, and I knew there was more she wished to say to me, only Edward's frowning presence prevented her.

"I don't know why you're so unbelieving," she whined. "Everyone knows that the spirits are about. We just need the right methods to contact them."

Uncle Phillip snorted and gave her his usual skeptical look. "The dead don't want the likes of you bothering them. The dead want to be left in peace."

For once Uncle Phillip made a good deal of sense. But Cousin Julia cast him a withering look. "I don't believe I've seen the devil lurking around any corners lately," she said with that irritating titter. "So it doesn't look like you've been all that successful at reaching him."

Uncle Phillip frowned. "Old Lucifer's a busy chap. He can't always be bothered to answer a summons."

"Perhaps —"

Edward slammed down his goblet so hard that wine splashed out on the table. "That will be enough!" he declared. "If you can't discuss ordinary, normal events, then don't converse at all. I'm sick to death of this petty battle between the two of you. Just as I'm sick of the peculiar beliefs you try to foist on me."

I was sick of it all, too, but I was even more shaken by the vehemence of my husband's remarks. Edward's temper — the temper I had hoped did not often make itself known seemed to be easily aroused, seemed almost to be waiting to be aroused. And that made me definitely uneasy.

But the rest of the meal passed in silence. Cousin Julia piled her plate high and emptied it — not once but three separate times. Uncle Phillip, too, ate heartily, though not the huge quantities Cousin Julia favored. Finally she pushed back her chair. "Excuse me," she murmured, darting a glance at Edward.

He nodded, his expression still grim.

Cousin Julia turned her gleaming eyes on me. "Would you care to walk with me a little?" she asked, her tone wheedling. Actually, I did not want to leave Edward's company. But Cousin Julia looked so woebegone, and the woman was alone in the world. She had no one except these relatives who barely tolerated her. So I, who was newly come to love and its joys, felt a wave of compassion roll over me.

"Yes, of course," I replied.

Cousin Julia smiled. "Shall we walk in the gallery?"

I had not yet been to the gallery so I nodded. She gathered her rose skirts about her like some huge pink ship about to set sail and started down the hall. I glanced at Edward, but he seemed intent on his food and did not respond to me.

Swallowing a sigh, I set out after Cousin Julia. I was much afraid I knew why she wanted me to walk with her, but perhaps I was wrong. "So," I said as we approached the gallery where the pictures of Edward's ancestors hung. "It's pleasant to walk after dinner, isn't it?"

Cousin Julia snorted. "I don't like walking," she said directly. "Never did Never will. I just wanted a chance to talk to you." She wrinkled her nose. "Edward is so fierce about my work with the spirits." She sighed heavily. "I can't understand why he doesn't want to talk to his dear departed papa. I should think he'd be eager."

She looked genuinely perplexed and I felt the time had come to declare myself. "Cousin Julia, Edward does not believe he *can* talk to his papa. Neither do I. In fact," I looked at her sternly, "it seems to me that trying to talk to the dead borders on sacrilege."

Cousin Julia's mouth rounded into a protesting O. "Indeed, it doesn't. Why, some of the best people talk to the dead! I assure you, it's quite the thing to do."

She was so confident, so sure of herself and her beliefs, that I felt my convictions shaken. But only slightly. Much as I might wish to speak to Jeremy once more, I could not wish for a world in which the souls of the departed must hover around the earth, hoping for a chance to speak to those left behind.

Jeremy was gone. I could not bring him back — but I wanted him to be at peace. I would remember that.

"This is the old earl's wife." Cousin Julia paused before a painting. "A beautiful woman, but out of her element here in this gloomy place."

I looked at the portrait. Edward's mother had indeed been a beautiful woman, with that warm golden beauty that seems to light a room. My heart skipped a beat. What was it Edward had said about Royale? That she was all sparkle and light. Like his mother, it seemed — at least superficially.

I sighed and moved on. I would never be fair, never have that warm golden glow that turned men's heads, that made them long to possess such ethereal beauty.

"And this is the old earl."

I stopped, rooted in place. The picture of

Edward's father needed no introduction. The resemblance was uncanny, so much so that I almost expected the man in the portrait to speak to me in Edward's deep tones.

I studied the picture closely and, as I did, I detected some differences. The man in the portrait had dark eyes like Edward's, but they were even colder, even harder than my husband's. I could not imagine those eyes warming with love, or even passion, though Edward had said his father was a man who much enjoyed the company of women.

The portrait seemed to hold my eyes. I knew Cousin Julia was staring at me, but I could not turn and meet her gaze.

"He was quite a man," she said, her voice full of more emotion than I had yet heard in it. "He had his faults, of course." She sniffled. "But he would never, never have taken his own life. I knew the man, knew him from childhood." Her voice turned grim. "He never ever gave up anything that was his. Not anything. He would not voluntarily give up his life."

Standing there, mesmerized by the eyes of the man in the portrait, I felt Cousin Julia was right. This hard, determined man had possessed great power. He had possessed power and he had reveled in it. He would not lightly have given it up.

I swallowed my sigh. In my bones I feared she was right. The former earl had not met death by his own hand. Someone had murdered him! And that someone was most probably still living in the castle.

Cousin Julia and I concluded our walk. I did not allow her to manipulate me into attending her séance. I knew Edward would disapprove of such a thing, but that was not the whole of it. I did not approve myself and so I saw no reason to go against my husband's expressed wishes.

We retired to my chamber early. He held me close for a moment, kissed me lightly, and said, "Good night, Hester." Then he was gone, through the adjoining door into *his* room.

And *my* room turned suddenly cold. I shivered and poked up the fire, but it did no good. I was chilled through and through, but not because of the cold. It was disappointment that made my flesh go clammy. Disappointment — and fear.

I didn't know exactly what I feared. But after I summoned Betty to help me prepare for bed, I sat before the dressing table, brushing my hair and wishing that I could be fair and sparkling, even hard as diamonds, if that was what my husband wanted.

But I knew I could not. Though I could be raised to ire when the fate of innocent children was involved, mine was a quiet nature, and, as he had said, peaceful. At least generally.

Feeling anything but peaceful, I threw down the brush and climbed into the big bed. But I left some candles burning. I wished for no more visits from clammy-handed ghosts.

Then I lay, staring up into the gloom, while my mind raced madly. If someone had murdered the old earl — and it certainly appeared that someone had — then why did they do it? What did they hope to profit from it?

In my mind I considered the inhabitants of the castle. Cousin Julia's penchant for spirits was unsettling, but she had seemed to feel genuine grief that the old earl was gone. And I did not see how she could have overcome the man or moved his body so as to hang from the chandelier.

Uncle Phillip's strange longing to see the devil face-to-face hardly made him a sane and sober citizen, but he was such a little stick of a man. I did not see how he could have moved the earl either.

I was not certain either of them was above murder, given the right circumstances, and that certainty had a chilling effect on me. But I simply could not see how either could have achieved the final position in which the old earl was found.

Now, Robert — that was different. Robert was a big man, hale and hardy. He could have overcome his father, could have arranged the whole thing to look like suicide. He had the most apparent motive. He'd been denied the earldom and he felt angry. Yes, Robert was the most likely person to have —

My heart almost stopped. I had left someone out of my reckoning. My husband, my husband who had succeeded to the earldom on the death of his father. My husband who had confessed to me that he hated that very father.

My head began to pound and my mouth went dry. Had I married a murderer? Could I now be carrying the unborn child of a madman?

I began to shiver in earnest then, mad, uncontrollable tremors that shook my body. I tried to get a grip on myself. It could not be. I could not have made such a horrible mistake.

I set myself to controlling my shaking body. I set my mind to calling up memories — tender, loving memories of Edward.

Holding me, kissing me, loving me. Could a murderer have behaved like that? No, no, I decided. I would not believe such an evil thing of my husband.

It must have been Robert. I would look into the matter. I would ask questions. After all, I had that right. I would find out who had done this horrible thing and bring him to justice. Then I would be free to love my husband. And the child to come. Our child.

Chapter Ten

The days passed. My new gowns arrived, rich, beautiful gowns befitting a countess. I wore them only to dinner.

Each day I spent time with the boys, teaching them lessons, but also trying to bring them to regard each other as friends. With the lessons, I had some success. With the friendship, I had none.

Though Ned and the twins both seemed to regard *me* in a friendly light, they were still suspicious and standoffish with each other. But I did not despair. I knew such things took time and I did feel that my presence had at least brought about an armed truce.

I spent my free time searching for the secret passageways and asking the servants what I hoped were subtle questions about the castle and its inhabitants, especially the former earl.

I did not find the passageways and I grew more and more convinced that if they existed the servants knew nothing of them. But when I began to talk about the inhabitants of the castle, it was a different story.

Every servant had some tale to relate, many about the old earl.

But, though they would talk, telling me stories about him, I sensed that there was more they weren't saying. And really the only new thing I learned was the disquieting information that the "old one," as they called him, had had quite a temper. This piece of news was hardly encouraging, coming as it did after the exhibitions of my husband's temper that I had witnessed.

But temper needn't mean madness — or murder. I told myself so repeatedly. And I believed it. Because in spite of all of my fears and uneasiness, my love for my husband was growing. Every day I seemed to love him more than I had the day before. It was not gratitude that made my body grow warm when I saw his beloved face and form, but something that went far deeper.

So things continued through the damp autumn. There was still no child growing of our love, but I was not unduly concerned about that. I felt deep in my soul that when the time was right, the child would be conceived.

One late November day, I was in the kitchen with Cook, discussing what would be planted in the kitchen garden come spring. And, perhaps because the thought just occurred to her, or perhaps because I had before evinced an interest in the previous earl, she began to tell me about the foods he liked.

"He were a man of definite tastes," she pronounced, slapping a handful of bread dough on the board. Her strong fingers kneaded in time to her words. "He liked his green onions, fresh from the garden. And his potatoes sprinkled with dill, just so."

She frowned. "Why, one day he threw a fit just 'cause we forgot the dill. He had such a temper. Threw those potatoes right against the wall — dish and all! Lord, what a mess!"

She nodded. "But his favorite dish was anise pudding." She wrinkled her nose. "It ain't to my taste, too bitter and all, but the old earl, he loved it. Had it the night he —"

Looking up from her kneading, Cook stopped abruptly in midsentence. Her eyes went round and I realized that someone stood in the doorway behind me, someone Cook didn't want to overhear her. But from the look on her face it was too late.

"Go on," Robert said abruptly. "Tell her the whole thing. He ate anise pudding the night he died."

Robert! If it was Robert Cook was afraid of, then maybe —

I turned and my heart sank. Edward stood beside his brother, his face grim. "That will be enough," he said, his voice cold. "You are not to discuss my father. Not at all. Is that clear?"

Cook bowed her head, her hands moving rhythmically in the dough. "Yes, milord. I won't, milord."

Robert laughed, a harsh sound, grating to the ears. "That's it," he said. "Play the heavy-handed lord." He turned a dazzling smile on me. "Keep it up and you'll soon drive Hester here away."

I knew my husband's various expressions, and I thought I glimpsed a shadow of doubt flit quickly across his face. Though when he turned to me, his countenance was blank, still I could not forbear replying to Robert.

"I am not easily driven away," I said crisply.

"Loyal Hester," Robert intoned darkly. "Let's hope your loyalty is not misplaced."

"Enough!" Edward barked. "I give you food and shelter, but I don't have to listen to your insults."

Robert looked about to reply again, but then he turned and stomped out. Edward was in no better case, his face crimson, his jaw tightly clenched. "Come," I said, drawing my arm through his. "Let's take a cup of tea in front of the fire. It's cozier there."

He allowed me to lead him out of the kitchen, but when we had reached the hall he stopped. "I cannot have tea now," he said, his voice devoid of all emotion. "I have an appointment in town."

I managed to keep my voice level too. "I see. And when do you expect to return?"

"I do not know." There was no warmth in his voice, no affection in his face. I might as well have been Hillyer, being informed of his departure like a servant.

A cold chill settled over me, and I pressed closer to Edward's side, hugging to me the arm that I had tucked mine through. "I shall hope that you finish your business in town and return in time for dinner," I said in my cheeriest tones. I smiled at him, too, hoping to elicit some answering warmth. But there was nothing. He was as cold as the stone walls — and just as unfeeling.

He pulled his arm free from my grasp. "I must go," he said.

His coldness unnerved me and I did what was for me quite an unusual thing. I threw myself into his arms. But even that evidence of affection brought no answering warmth. He simply set me aside. Like a piece of furniture or a cloak he no longer wanted, he set me aside and walked out.

I stared after him, his name rising to my lips. I opened my mouth to call out to him, to beg him to stay, but I closed it again without uttering a sound. I had always been a proud person — and after his rebuff I could not bring myself to plead.

And so I stood in stunned silence until my husband was out of sight. Then I felt a rising anger that I should be so foully treated! How could the man love me so tenderly and then treat me so coldly? It made no sense.

Neither did my anger, but it would not dissipate, and finally, in desperation, I took my hooded cloak and set out for a walk. Since our first walk together I had not gone often abroad. The weather had turned cold soon after our arrival and I had been busy with the boys.

Besides, I did not like to venture on the moor alone. Edward had warned me that it was an easy matter to lose one's way there on the land that, though it looked flat, was deceptively rolling and could cut off distant views when one least expected it.

But now I did not care for warnings or for anything else. The castle seemed to be closing in on me, its chill reaching to my very bones, its air fetid and numbing. I had to get out of there.

A brisk walk, I told myself, would restore my spirits. But I knew differently. It was going to take more than a walk to make me accept my husband's treatment of me with any aplomb. And if he did not come to my bed that night, if he left me to sleep alone —

I dared not think such thoughts. Pulling my cloak tighter around me, I hurried down the path. The winter air was more than brisk, it was dank and cold, but I preferred it to being shut up in the castle.

I made my way through the twisted trees, walking carefully because the snow-covered ground was damp and slippery. I tried to concentrate on keeping my footing, but my thoughts reverted to my husband and his peculiar behavior. Why did he vacillate so toward me — one moment passionate and loving, the next cold and distant? Could he be like the old earl, a man whose passion for women was almost legendary, but who, from what I'd been able to gather, used and then discarded them?

A shudder sped over me, a shudder that had little to do with the cold air of winter. Could my Edward be like his father? Like his brother, Robert? Would my husband tire of me and look to take his pleasure in another's bed?

The thought brought a sob to my throat

and tears to my eyes. I didn't think I could stand the pain of such a thing. I blinked and tried to clear my vision.

Then I struggled to take myself in hand. My imaginings were farfetched, I told myself sternly. Perhaps Edward had something serious on his mind today, perhaps tonight he would be his former self — loving and passionate, yet gentle. After all, he had apologized for his harshness before.

I looked up, blinking back the tears, determined to concentrate on the scenery around me. The wood was growing darker. The trees, though not towering, reached high enough so that their twisted, tangled branches hid most of the sky. The wood was bathed in dark shadows so I surmised that clouds were then covering the sun.

I shivered. I should return to the castle before I got a chill, but first I wanted to reach the end of the path through the oaks, to gaze for a moment on the peaceful beauty of the moor.

It took me only a few more minutes. Then I stood at the edge of the wood and caught my breath. Even in winter the moor had an untrammeled beauty. I stepped forward, wanting to see a little farther, to absorb the sense of peace and beauty that seemed to hang in the still air.

I took a few steps, then a few more, but mindful of Edward's cautions about getting lost, I went no farther than ten feet from the edge of the wood. There I stopped, drinking in the pristine beauty, the peaceful silence —

The silence was broken by a familiar sound, that of a galloping horse. I swung around, thinking that Ned was returning from a ride, but it was not Ned approaching me. The sun behind him blinded me, allowing me to see only a rider on a dark horse, a rider so cloaked and hatted as to be unrecognizable to me.

There was no time to think. Even as I watched, the rider put the spurs to his great black horse and the animal sprang straight for me.

In panic I turned, trying to make the shelter of the wood, thinking the twisted trees would protect me. But the ground was wet and my shoe caught in the hem of my cloak, hurling me into the wet snow.

I could see the trees; their safety was only a few paces away. I scrambled to my hands and knees, trying to get to my feet. The horse was almost upon me, the pounding of its hooves thudding in my ears. My breath was coming in great gasps, my legs would hardly support me, but I kept my eyes on the trees, the twisted contorted trees that meant protection.

Then the horse was upon me. In one last effort I lunged toward the wood. The horse galloped by, hitting me a striking blow that threw me into the edge of the wood. And then they were gone, horse and rider pounding off over the moor.

I lay in the wet snow where I had been thrown, trying to pull breath into my tortured lungs, trying to assure myself that I was still alive. There was no doubt in my mind that the horseman had seen me. The sun had been at his back, and my dark cloak had made me stand out against the snow.

As my breathing gradually slowed I faced the frightening truth. Someone had tried to run me down! Perhaps to kill me!

Shaking, I pushed myself to my feet. My gown and my cloak were muddy and wet. My teeth were chattering from the cold and my limbs trembling in the aftermath of fear. Why? Why should someone try to kill me?

True, there had been that eerie voice that urged me to leave the castle. And the clammy hand that had touched my cheek in the darkness. But that had been weeks ago, when I first came to Grey Cliffs. Nothing like that had happened since.

I started back toward the castle, but I

staggered and had to reach out to a tree for support. Somehow the touch of the bark reminded me of the kitchen, of Cook kneading dough and telling me about the old earl's last meal.

The hair stood up on the back of my neck. This attack had been made upon me shortly after Edward and his brother found me discussing their father with Cook. Had she said something that someone thought might help me discover the old earl's killer?

A gust of cold, salt-laden wind hit me and I shivered again. I'd better get back to the castle before I took a real chill. Otherwise nature might well finish the task the horseman had bungled.

I managed to get in through the kitchen entrance without being seen and hurried up the backstairs to my room. I didn't want anyone to see me because I hadn't yet decided if I would mention this attack. I did not like to be suspicious of my husband. But I could not be entirely sure of his love. And until I was —

I pushed open the door to my room and slipped into its dimness. Breathing a sigh of relief at being safe, I turned.

And then I gasped. Standing in the door to his room, holding a candelabra, was

Edward. "Where have you been?" he demanded gruffly.

"I went for a walk."

He raised an eyebrow. "In this weather?"

"Yes, Edward, in this weather." My usual calm spirits seemed to have forsaken me. My patience was exhausted. I was cold and wet — and angry. I took off my cloak and dropped it, a sodden mess, to the floor.

Edward came closer, setting the candelabra on the table. He reached for me.

"I missed —" he began. "God. God, Hester! You're soaking wet!"

"I fell."

His fingers tightened on my arms. "Fell? How?"

Standing so close to him, still I could not suspect him. I moved into his arms. "A rider, a man, tried to run me down. The horse hit me and knocked me over."

"People should be more careful," Edward said. "And you, what were you doing on the road?"

"I was not on the road," I returned. "I was standing on the moor, just at the edge of the wood. And he rode right at me."

I felt Edward's body go tense. His arms tightened around me till I could hardly breathe. "Hester! My God! Were you hurt?"

"No, only frightened." I shivered, even

there in the safety of his arms. "But it seemed like he meant to kill me." I gulped. "Oh, Edward, why should someone try to kill *me?*"

My husband was silent for a moment, clasping me to him. "It can't be that," he said finally, his voice muffled in my hair. "It was probably some youngster, you know how they are. Looking to stir up some excitement. After all, he didn't come back. He didn't trample you."

Edward was right about that. And yet I knew that this had not been some young man's boyish prank. There had been about that horseman an air of deliberate, malicious intent.

But while I debated trying to explain this to my husband, he turned me around and undid my hooks. "Come," he said, leading me to the washstand. "Let's get some of that mud off you. And then we'll warm you up."

By the time Edward had finished washing me off and taken me into the great bed to warm me in the way most favored by husbands and wives, I had almost forgotten the horseman and my horrible experience. It was not until some time later, several days in fact, that I realized that Edward had never explained to me the reason for his cold behavior that fateful afternoon.

Chapter Eleven

The next day I came upon the twins in heated conversation. They were using their private language. Though unknown to them I had been able to piece together some of it, I was unable to make out what had so excited them.

Ned, playing ball with the dog in a corner of the nursery, seemed to have no interest in them at all. Until Paul slipped over to him and whispered something I couldn't hear.

Ned looked up, his face alight, and a sudden chill danced down my spine. I could think of only one thing that would excite the boy like that. The twins had found the secret passageway!

But if they had, they were not going to tell me.

"Can we go out to the stable?" Ned asked. "We like to play out there."

"Of course," I returned. Pretending ignorance, I watched them get their jackets and set out. But I knew quite well that their destination was not the stable. Moments later, I slipped out the door. Lingering in the shadows, I listened for the sound of their youthful voices.

To the right, I decided. I headed in that direction, the direction of the portrait gallery, carefully keeping to the shadows.

There was little need for me to take care, however. The boys were so excited with their find that they forgot to keep their voices down and never once looked behind them.

I kept to the shadows and drew closer. As I did I saw that the full-length portrait of the old earl had been swung out, away from the wall. Evidently it was set upon some kind of hinges. And beside it the excited boys peered into a black hole. I was right! They had found the entrance to the passageway!

I debated my next course of action. Should I slip away and pretend I knew nothing of the matter? Or should I accost them? The blackness of the hole decided me. I could not let them venture into such a dangerous place alone.

I stepped out of the shadows. "So," I said sternly. "This is how you obey the earl."

The twins dropped their gaze, lowering their heads submissively, but Ned faced me defiantly. "My father's not fair," he cried. "He brought me to live in this castle! I want to know all about it."

I looked into Ned's reddening face and said calmly, "But he did not tell you about the priest hole." I was only guessing, but I believed I was right. Edward had made it plain that he wanted no one to search for the secret passageways. And knowing his son as he did, he would not have told him stories that would impel the boy to undertake such a search.

No, someone else had told Ned about the passageways and the priest hole and the dry bones. I bent down to look into the absolute darkness of the hole in the wall. It was so black in there, blacker than the blackest midnight. The air was stale, fetid. In spite of myself, I shuddered.

I straightened and drew back. "We cannot go in there without a light. It's impossible to see."

Grinning, Paul produced a handful of candles from his pockets. I held back a smile. One day soon Hillyer would be wondering what had happened to deplete his supply of candles.

Paul took one and scurried off to hold it to the candelabra at the end of the gallery. When he came back, he lit a candle for each of us.

"We must stay together," I said firmly. I knew Edward would disapprove of us doing this. But I also knew there was no way I could keep these excited boys from ex-

153

ploring their find. Since I could not stop them, and I could not let them go in there alone, I must go with them. This I told myself, preparing, as it were, the explanation I would give Ned's father.

The passageway was pitch black, the entrance a frightful darkness even in the gloomy gallery. The boys hung back, and I sensed fear mingled with their excitement. For myself, I felt more fear than anything else. But I took a step forward, into that black void. And immediately something struck, clung to my face.

It was only by biting down hard on my bottom lip that I stifled the scream that rose in my throat.

"Cobwebs," Ned said gleefully. "There's cobwebs all over in here."

I let my breath out in a sigh of relief. Holding my candle high, I saw that Ned was right. The passageway was festooned with cobwebs. We brushed them aside as we moved farther on.

Paul turned to pull the portrait shut behind us. As the gallery faded from our sight, I shivered. If we should get lost in this terrible place —

"Set the candle in front of the doorway out," I told Peter. "That way we can find our way back."

Peter did as I'd suggested and lit another candle. Then we moved on down the passageway, a silent band of explorers. After a few minutes, when nothing untoward happened, the boys began to regain their usual good spirits.

"I bet this leads to the priest hole," Ned said, satisfaction in his voice. "If we find that, we'll have a secret hiding place." He turned to me. "If Hester doesn't tell on us."

Until that moment, the possibility of keeping the boys' find a secret had not dawned on me. But I realized that Edward was going to blame me. No matter that I hadn't initiated this search. I had not stopped them from pursuing it. I had accompanied them. And where before I had merely *seen* Edward's temper — and it not directed at me — this time I was sure to bear the brunt of his rage.

Still, that was not sufficient reason to lie to my husband. "We shall see," I said to Ned. "By the way, I thought you were going to the stable."

Ned looked sheepish. "We were, after a bit. We want to look at the new horse Father got."

"A new horse," I repeated, more to keep the boy talking than anything else, since horses were hardly my favorite topic.

"Yes," Ned said. "A big one. Black as this old hole."

A cold hand seemed to clutch my heart. A black horse. The man that had almost run me down had ridden a black horse. And Edward had been away from the house when it happened. Could my husband, that I loved so much, have tried to kill me?

I stopped in the passageway, gasping for breath as the awful thought hit me. But why? Why would Edward — or anyone else — try to kill me?

And the answer came, the only answer possible. I knew something, something that pointed to the old earl's killer. Something that might unmask him. But what was it?

"Hester?" Ned was pulling at my sleeve anxiously. "Are you sick?"

"No. No, Ned. I'm all right. I just wanted to rest for a minute."

We pressed on then, and I made up my mind. For now at least, I would not tell Edward we'd found the passageway. It was not to escape his anger, but because I was afraid — afraid that the attack upon me at the edge of the wood might have come from the person I loved most in the world.

The passageway ran on for what seemed a very long time, finally ending in a little wooden door.

"I knew it!" Ned cried. "We found it — the priest hole!"

And indeed we had. The door opened with a slight creak and there beyond it was a dark dismal room. Poor priest, I thought, who must hide in such a hole. With no light and little air.

"Oh!" breathed the twins.

"What a place!" Ned cried. "A great hiding hole!"

At first I was minded to forbid the boys the place. But I took my candle and made a circuit of the little room. It took very little time, since it was more hole than actual room. And I saw that there was no way they could be hurt here. There were no windows to fall out of. And with walls and floor of cold, bare stone, nothing to be set afire. The passageway led straight to the place. There was no way to get lost.

I turned to face them. "I know you will want to play here."

Three youthful faces looked to me with mingled hope and despair.

"I will allow it," I said finally.

The twins hugged each other and Ned actually hugged me.

"But there are some rules to observe," I went on.

"Oh, we will," said the twins together.

"Me, too," Ned cried.

"First, no one must come in here alone." They all nodded. "Second, you must always leave a candle at the portrait door."

"Of course."

"And third, you must not follow the passageway in the other direction."

They nodded in unison. I breathed a sigh of relief. "I will not tell anyone about this place," I said. "*If* you obey the rules. If you do not —"

"We will!" Ned hastened to say. "Oh, we will. Hester —" The boy looked at me and his face twisted as though he were undergoing some inner struggle. "I — I'm glad you came here," he said finally.

I smiled. "So am I," I said. And, though my heart was troubled by the things I'd discovered, I meant it. I was glad to be at Grey Cliffs. I was also afraid.

It was several days later that I found myself alone with Ned. Betty had taken the twins off to the village to see some old friends. I sat by the nursery fire, a book in my lap, and Ned played on the hearth with the dog.

"You really like dogs, don't you?" I said.

Ned nodded. "And horses." He looked up, his eyes shining. "They run so fast! It's wonder — Hester, what is it? What's wrong?"

In spite of myself I had let my face betray me. The mention of horses not only recalled my mother's fatal accident but also the incident on the moor. "I — I'm all right," I said.

Ned frowned. "You looked so scared." He thought for a moment. "Hester, are you afraid of horses?"

I thought about lying, but the boy would discover my secret eventually. Perhaps my telling him would engender some trust. "Yes," I said. "I am. Very much afraid."

"But, Hester, horses are so marvelous. So big and fast and —"

"One ran away with our carriage," I explained, "when I was younger than you. And my mother was killed."

Ned left the dog and came to put his arms around me. "I'm sorry. I bet you miss her."

"I do," I agreed. "Very much." I returned his hug. "As you must miss your mother."

The boy stiffened. "I don't —" Then he crumpled. "I miss her a lot," he said. "But I'm not supposed to talk about her."

"You can talk to me," I said. "About anything."

He sniffled. "I don't miss her so much since you came. You treat me nicer than she did." He drew back and looked me in the eye. "Hester, you don't have to be afraid of horses. They don't hurt you on purpose."

Something in the boy's face told me that people had hurt him. And he thought it was done on purpose.

"The thing is," Ned went on. "They get afraid, too, horses do, so then you have to move slowly. Let's go out to the stables. I'll show you and —"

"We'll see," I said hastily. I didn't want to go to the stables. I didn't want to see the new black horse, or any horse for that matter.

"I'd be —"

The twins appeared in the doorway, with Betty behind them. Ned gave me a conspiratorial look. "Just remember," he said and went back to the dog.

And I did remember. I knew Ned had given me good advice, but I did not follow it. I had too much else on my mind to consider my fear of horses pressing. And that was another mistake.

Chapter Twelve

The days continued to pass. The boys kept their discovery of the passageway a secret, even from Betty. I was pleased by that because I didn't see how the little maid could keep such word to herself. The servants were already very superstitious, whispering about seeing the ghost of the old earl and casting fearful looks over their shoulders wherever they went. If it were known, talk of such a passageway would spread rapidly and sooner or later Edward would hear of it.

I did not want that to happen. Things between us had been quite good. Since the day the horseman had attacked me on the moor, Edward had been most attentive. It was true that sometimes he was quiet, moody, even withdrawn. But he was never angry — at least not with me.

Still, much as I loved my husband, my nerves were on edge. I had the weirdest feeling that someone was watching me. Yet when I had that feeling I was always by myself, in my room or some other part of the castle. Sometimes I even whirled, thinking to catch someone there behind me. But there was never anyone there. Always I was alone. And yet always I *felt* that I was not.

Evidently the strain began to tell on me. One night about a week after the incident on the moor, Edward and I had gone up to our chamber early and were lying the great bed talking.

Edward touched my cheek tenderly. "Hester, my love, you are looking peaked. Is something wrong? Are you feeling ill?"

"No," I said, pressing his hand to my lips. I paused, but I knew I should go on. "It's just that I have been hearing strange stories — about your father's ghost."

Edward snorted. "You know how servants are. They repeat every ridiculous story — and embellish it, too."

"Perhaps. But that doesn't account for the feeling I have — the feeling that I'm being watched."

His face paled. Even in the candlelight I could see that. "You're letting your imagination carry you away," he said. "No one can be watching you. How can you say such a thing?"

"I say it because I *feel* it," I replied. I hesitated, then forced myself to go on. "Edward?"

He traced the contour of my cheek, his fingers so warm, so tender. "Yes, love?"

"Do you think — Could it be —" I gulped. "Could your father be —"

Edward clasped me to him and even in my fear I felt my body respond to his. "Hester, there are no ghosts. Surely you know that."

"Perhaps not," I said, my lips against his chest. "But I know how I feel. And last week — on the moor — that was no boy playing pranks. That was a grown man! I know he tried to run me down!"

Edward's hard male body stiffened against mine. The silence in the room lengthened and lengthened. Finally he spoke. "Hester! My darling Hester. You must be mistaken. No one would want to harm you."

He seemed so sure that I did not try to persuade him otherwise. Besides, then he crushed me to him, his mouth covering mine with such passion that my body responded immediately. Still, even then, even as my body heated to his caresses, there remained the niggling questions in the back of my mind.

Why did Edward refuse to believe me? Why did he want to persuade me that I was not in any danger?

But there in his arms I felt so safe, so secure, that soon even the questions were forgotten.

When he left my bed next morning, Edward turned to me with a frown. "Hester."

"Yes, Edward?" I stirred sleepily, gazing up at him with a fond smile.

His voice grew stern. "Do not ask the servants any more questions about my father."

"But Cousin Julia says —"

"Forget Cousin Julia!" Edward barked. "My father is dead. Dead!"

"Yes, Edward, I know." I was coming awake in a hurry, losing all my good feelings of joy and love. "But I was only trying to find out what —"

"Hester! Listen to me!" His voice grew harsher, full of rage.

No answering anger rose in me. Rather I felt a coldness sweep over me, a terrible coldness that struck to the bone. In his anger, Edward frightened me.

Thinking to appease him, I began again. "I only want to know —"

Edward turned back to the bed. His fingers closed around my wrist. In one swift movement he dragged me from the bed's safety to stand naked before him, shivering on the cold stone floor.

"No more!" he cried. And he shook me savagely. Once. Twice. I bit my bottom lip to keep from crying out at this indignity, but still a little whimper escaped me.

He stopped abruptly, his fierce expression fading to one of tenderness. "Hester, please, for God's sake! Don't pursue this thing."

And then to my utter bafflement, he lifted me tenderly in his arms and carried me to the bed, where with the utmost gentleness he put me down and pulled the coverlet up.

He stood, towering over me, a dark, faceless figure with the sunlight behind him. I thought with sudden fear of the horseman galloping toward me across the moor.

Edward was strong, said a voice in my head, a voice I could not silence. So powerful he could have shaken me into insensibility. So strong he could easily have moved the deadweight of an unconscious man.

Trembling overtook me then and I shivered between the sheets that were still warm from his beloved body.

He bent and dropped an affectionate kiss on my forehead, whispering, "God, Hester, if anything happened to you, I couldn't bear it."

A great rush of tenderness enfolded me — and with it a greater sense of shame. How could I have doubted this man who cared so much for me? The man in whose arms I had experienced so much passion? The man whose child might even that moment be growing within me?

Then he was gone, hurrying off to attend to estate business, and I was left to my usual pursuits.

Late that afternoon, when lessons were over, I decided to take a short walk. I loved the boys dearly, but their continual company could be trying and sometimes I longed for a little peace and quiet, a little time just to myself.

Since it was late in the day and the light would soon be waning, I decided not to walk through the twisted oaks. Besides, I had no desire to be on the moor again — not alone at least.

But I did feel the need for some fresh air. So I took my hooded cloak from Hillyer and went out, walking around the castle. I had not yet been on the path that led to the cliffs beneath my window, the cliffs that overlooked the sea.

The sea, with its shifting moods, had always fascinated me. And I had always held a fondness for high places. The latter, perhaps, because of having followed a youthful Jeremy up many a tree. So that afternoon I stood entranced on the edge of the grey cliffs that gave the castle its name and stared down at the gleaming rocks below.

The sun had come out from behind the clouds and was lighting the sea. Glistening like ebony beneath the washing waves, the rocks below glowed with shimmering beauty.

But I was not deceived. Beautiful though they might appear, the rocks were also deadly. A slip off that cliff would be the end. No one could hope to survive such a brutal fall. No one.

The sun slid behind a cloud again, throwing the castle and the sea into dark shadow. Where before the sea had seemed inviting, sparkling and beautiful, now it threatened, cold and deadly. Instinctively I took a step backward.

And then I heard it. What sounded like the whine of a shell passing close by my head was followed almost immediately by the report of a pistol being fired.

Without even thinking, I fell to my knees, my heart leaping up in my throat. Thank God for the cloud and its shadow. The instinctive backward step had saved my life. Had I been standing right on the edge of the cliff when the shot startled me —

I sank lower still, huddling against the ground. But I was aware that I was all too visible, my black cloak against the grey rocks making me a clear target. I had no idea where he was and there was no cover near me. Completely at the attacker's mercy, I waited.

But no second shot came. Finally, slowly, I got to my feet and left the cliffs. But I could not leave behind the knowledge that this had been no accident. Someone had tried to kill me. Again!

By the time I reached the front of the castle I was out of breath, but my trembling had ceased. I rearranged my clothing and tried to pull my countenance into an everyday expression. If only I had someone to confide in, someone to help me.

Of course, my first thought was to tell Edward, but he was still gone from the castle. And he had refused to believe that the rider on the moor meant me harm. Would he believe that someone had shot at me? Or would he try to pass off this, too, as a youthful prank or perhaps a figment of my imagination? I could not understand why, when he seemed so concerned for my well-being, he refused to acknowledge these attempts on my life.

I reached the front door and gave my cloak into Hillyer's waiting hands. "The earl has just returned," he said. "He inquired as to your whereabouts."

My heart thudded in my throat. "Where is the earl now?"

Hillyer's expression remained composed. "I believe he went out to look for you."

My heart threatened to leap out of my mouth. Edward had known I was gone out for a walk. Edward could have — *Stop it!* I told myself severely. Edward would not do such a thing. He would not.

I started up the stairs, intent on reaching my room and freshening up before I faced my husband's discerning eyes. But I was not quite to the top when the front door opened again.

I paused. If I saw Edward, if I felt his strong arms around me, I could shake these nagging suspicions. I started to turn. But Edward was not alone.

"I told you, Robert," he snapped. "Nothing till quarter day. And if you've caused any more trouble in the village, there'll be nothing even then."

The front door closed with a thud. "You're a fool!" Robert cried, his tone sending chills over my flesh. "I'll have what's mine. One way or another, I'll have what's mine!"

I waited no longer, but hurried on up the stairs before either of them saw me.

Was it Robert? Could Robert be trying to kill me? To take some sort of revenge against the brother he thought was keeping his rightful inheritance from him?

But if it had been Robert, why hadn't he finished the job? That day on the moor I had been completely alone, defenseless. The horseman could have returned and easily dispatched me. And on the cliffs I had had no cover. He could have fired a second shot — a second shot that would have surely ended my life.

In the safety of my chamber I washed my face and tidied my clothes. My new gowns were lovely, but I could not appreciate the beauty of the sea-green silk I changed into.

I thought instead about the peculiar inhabitants of this castle. Which of them had stood to gain the most by killing the old earl? Which of them now wanted me and my questions out of the way?

Edward, of course, had been the one to inherit the title. But I refused to consider that the man I'd married, the man I'd come to love, could be a murderer. If a murderer existed in this castle, it had to be someone else.

Robert seemed likely. He was obviously angry at Edward for withholding his allowance. And he was next in line for the earlship. But that did not explain the attacks on me — or the old earl's murder. From what I could gather, Robert had felt some affection for the father that he was so much like. And killing him had only put Edward in power, it had not helped Robert.

I shook the pins out of my hair and began to redress it. What about Cousin Julia? What did she stand to gain? Her position in the castle depended on the present earl's generosity. No laws required those in power to provide for their less fortunate relations. But Cousin Julia seemed to have held a certain affection for the old earl, and surely if *she* had dispatched him, she would not keep telling people that he had been murdered.

I shook my head in frustration. The whole thing was such a tangle. What about Uncle Phillip? What had he gained from the old earl's demise? As far as I could tell, very little. He was far removed from the line of succession and his pastimes, eccentric as they might be, had so far as I could discern not met with the old earl's disapproval.

There were the servants, too. Of course I could not really imagine that one of them had dared to murder the old earl. Though there was something about Hillyer that inspired a certain dislike in me, I could not picture the man as a killer.

I sighed, inspected my redressed hair in the glass, and rose. I had no proof that the old earl had been murdered. Perhaps all that had happened since was coincidence. Still, my heart told me differently.

Too much had occurred. Someone wanted me to stop asking questions. But how could I? If the old earl *had* been murdered, the murderer was still at large. And if he had killed once, he might well kill again. I could not allow such a state of affairs to continue. I had the children to think of.

Chapter Thirteen

Satisfied that my appearance gave no hint of this second attack on my person, and wanting to avoid my husband's scrutiny, I went to look for the boys. I found Betty in the nursery — alone. As usual, she was close by the fire, humming under her breath. She looked up from her mending, smiling brightly and nodding. "Milady."

I looked around the room. "Where are the boys?"

Betty grinned. "Them scamps is off playing. They likes to play tag in the portrait gallery, it being so long and all. Poor tikes, 'tis hard on 'em now that the weather's turned cold. Boys has such high spirits. They must always be up and doing something, you know."

I nodded, but knew with chilling certainty that the boys were not playing tag in the gallery. They had probably gone into the secret passageway, to play games in the priest hole.

The thought made my heart begin to pound. Edward was already very angry. If he found the boys in the passageway, in defiance of his express orders, he would be incensed. He might even turn the twins out, to live who knew how. I could not allow such a thing to happen.

"Fine," I mumbled, picking up a candle and turning hastily away. "I'll just go watch."

The portrait gallery was some distance from the nursery and by the time I reached it I was out of breath. It was deserted, of course, gloomy in the scant afternoon light. I hurried up to the painting of the old earl. Glancing around, I made sure there was no servant nearby to see me. Then with one hand I held my candle and with the other I tugged at the portrait.

Slowly it opened. Well back from the portal, a single candle flickered in its holder on the floor. I let out my breath in a sigh of relief. Evidently the boys *had* gone to the priest hole. With any luck I could get them safely out, undiscovered, before Edward knew anything of it.

Holding my candle carefully, I pulled the portrait closed behind me. The corridor was almost free of cobwebs now, but with the portrait in place the narrow walls closed in on me, making it hard for me to breathe — to think. Under normal circumstances I would not have entered this frightening place alone. But my fear for the twins' future made me braver. I had to find the boys, find them and get them back to the nursery before Edward discovered what they were about.

I had gone perhaps thirty or forty paces, trying to keep my nerves calm, trying to tell myself all would be well, when I heard the noise behind me. First the sound of footsteps. And then a laugh — a sinister, demonic laugh. The hair on the back of my neck stood up and gooseflesh rose on my arms. The ghost! The ghost had followed me into the passageway!

I whirled, holding the candle high, frantically searching the darkness behind me. But I could see nothing. The feeble rays of the candle reached only a few feet. Beyond them loomed terrifying blackness.

I stood frozen. Should I retrace my steps, go back to the portrait, and perhaps confront the ghost? Or should I seek refuge in the priest hole where the boys were playing?

I wanted nothing more than to be out of there, safe and secure, in the portrait gallery beyond the portal to the passageway. But to get there I must go through that awful blackness, risk meeting with the demonic laughter.

My knees began to tremble violently. I took one step back toward the portal. Another step. The laughter sounded again, beating against my eardrums in a mad cadence that made me want to scream and strike out at the elusive darkness.

With a sob, I whirled and fled toward the questionable safety of the priest hole and the children.

Moments later, completely out of breath, I pushed open the door and practically fell into the little room. An awful sight greeted me.

The priest hole was empty. Small and unfurnished as it was, it offered absolutely no hiding places. The boys just were not there.

I slammed the door shut, sagging against it while I fought to catch my breath. Could ghosts come through doors? The very outlandishness of the question startled me back to sensibility. Remember the footsteps. I had to remember that there were no ghosts.

The thought, however, offered little comfort. A real person, the old earl's murderer, for example, could be far more dangerous to me than any ghost.

I leaned all my weight against the door, but I was not a heavy woman. How could *I* keep someone out? Someone who wanted to get in, who wanted to get *me?*

The candle trembling in my hand showed me nothing in the room that I could use to defend myself. Oh why had I come into this place? And where were the boys?

The thought of the children made new terror strike at my heart. Had whoever was out there taken the children? If they had been harmed I would never forgive myself.

What should I do? Should I open the door and confront whatever was out there? Should I go back down the passageway to the gallery? But what of the boys?

I couldn't think. I could hardly even breathe. I was feeling so weak I was afraid my knees would give way. I trembled violently. What was I to do?

And then I heard voices — cheerful laughing voices. The most wonderful sound in this dismal place. I straightened. And they were coming closer! I moved to one side and slowly opened the door.

I heaved a sigh of relief. The boys were coming down the passageway — Ned, with Captain at his heels, leading the way.

"Hester!" he cried. "What are you doing here?"

I pulled myself together, willed my voice to calmness. "I was looking for you. Your father has come home."

Ned paled, losing some of his bravado. "We'd better go back to the nursery then."

"Yes," I said. "And right away."

The boys were silent as we made our way back to the candle that marked the portal. I stared down at it, then at the blackness that extended behind it, blackness that led into other parts of the passageway. With shock I realized where they had been.

I faced the boys. "You went into the other passageways after I told you not to."

Ned frowned but he didn't hesitate. "Yes, Hester. But we heard someone there! And I had Captain so I knew no one could hurt us." The dog growled, as though reinforcing the boy's words.

For the moment I did not comment on their disregard of my rules. "Did you find anyone?"

The three shook their heads. "No," Ned said. "But the passageways go all over the castle." His face brightened. "Want to see?"

I shook my head. I had no desire to see any more of secret passageways.

"We were going out then," Paul said.

"But Captain wouldn't go," Peter continued.

Ned nodded emphatically. "He kept whining and whining. And going toward the priest hole." He smiled. "He must have known you were there."

"Perhaps." I wondered if the dog had indeed known I was in danger. I stooped to pat his head and mentally promised him a good big bone.

Then I straightened. We could waste no more time. "Listen carefully. You must get back to the nursery now." I fixed them with a cold eye. "We will talk later about this disobedience of yours."

After I saw the boys safely back in Betty's care, I returned to my room for another inspection of my person. I told myself it would not do to appear with cobwebs in my hair, but in reality I was simply loath to face Edward. I was afraid that he might sense, that he might read in my eyes, the suspicions of him that I could not entirely erase.

I loved him. I knew that. I loved him very much. But I would not be the first woman to be betrayed by her senses, to see in a man only what she wanted to see. I swallowed a sob and turned from the mirror. Edward could not be the killer. He simply could not.

I straightened my shoulders. When I saw him again, all my doubts about him would vanish. Then I would be sure once more.

I moved slowly down the great stairs, the silk of my new gown whispering against the stones. But the sound of it was soon drowned by other sounds. "What do you mean you don't know?" Edward was roaring.

"Milord —" For the first time I detected emotion in Hillyer's voice. "The countess came in some minutes ago. She didn't inform me what she intended to do next."

"Find her!" Edward shouted. "Find her now!"

I swallowed over the lump in my throat and hurried toward them. "That won't be necessary," I called. "I am coming down now."

Edward and the butler stared up at me. Edward was clearly distraught, the butler obviously discomposed.

Edward bounded up the stairs toward me. "Hester! My God, where have you been?" He crushed me to him so tightly I could scarcely breathe.

"I went for a walk," I said, as calmly as I could. "And then I went to check on the children." Though it was not exactly a lie, still it stuck in my throat.

"When I couldn't find you —" Edward shuddered. "I thought —"

"What did you think?" Cousin Julia's words came out of the darkness behind me, startling me so that, tightly as Edward held me, I still jumped. Edward gathered me closer.

"Did you think your father's ghost had gotten her?" Cousin Julia asked, punctuating her words with a shrill titter.

I shivered. Why had Cousin Julia chosen that precise moment to mention the old earl's ghost? Had *she* been in the passageway, uttering that uncanny laugh

Edward's face had gone white. I heard the hiss of his indrawn breath, felt his body stiffen as he fought to control his temper. Finally he was able to speak. "I do not believe in ghosts," he said, his voice cold. "As you well know."

I did not want any more of this baiting. "Come," I said, "let's go down to the library and have some tea. I am very thirsty."

Edward released me, but kept his arm tucked through mine. "Of course, my dear."

As we descended the stairs, I knew that I could not tell him about the shot that had been fired at me. Not then at least. Certainly not while Cousin Julia was hanging about like some fat leech ready to fasten upon him.

My doubts about him had not vanished and I was confused by my vague feelings of suspicion.

My thoughts distressed me so that by the time we had reached the library I really did need a cup of tea. What was making Edward act so strangely? Did he know something I did not?

Cousin Julia rang for Hillyer, then took her usual chair, closest to the fire.

When the butler appeared, Edward looked to me. "A pot of hot tea," I said.

Hillyer nodded. "Yes, milady."

"And a plate of tea cakes," Cousin Julia added shrilly. "A big plate."

Hillyer looked again to me and I nodded. The grim-faced butler knew that I was mistress of this place. It was a small victory, but sweet.

Unfortunately I did not have long to enjoy it. Robert and Uncle Phillip came in together, Uncle Phillip's carpet slippers slapping against the stone floor, his breeches as usual covered with dust. Considering the ill-assorted inhabitants of the castle, it was a good thing we had few callers. I swallowed a sigh. I could have used a good friend, a female confidante.

Cousin Julia, however, did not seem a good choice. I seriously doubted she could long keep any information private. And since she already found the old earl's death suspicious, she was sure to make much ado about these attempts on my life. *If* they were attempts. Perhaps the perpetrator had meant only to frighten me, to make me back off.

Round and round my thoughts circled.

But always I was left with the same dilemma. Who could be doing these things?

"You're looking lovely tonight, Hester." Robert paused before me and was looking down, admiration in his eyes.

"Thank you," I replied, as civilly as I could. "It's the new gown, one of those Edward got me." I sent my husband a smile, but he was scowling. Certainly he could see that I had not invited his brother's attentions.

I had long ago divined that Robert was the sort who played up to anything in skirts. I did not let his behavior mean anything to me.

I kept smiling at Edward and ignoring his brother, and finally my husband smiled back.

Uncle Phillip plopped into a chair. "Could use some tea," he said. "It's dusty work I'm doing."

"Tea's coming," Cousin Julia announced before I could speak. She pulled herself erect in her chair. "Don't know why you toy with those dusty old books when summoning the spirits is so easy."

Uncle Phillip snorted and rolled his eyes. "How many times must I tell you, you silly old woman. I am not interested in spirits." His eyes twinkled. "It's the head man I want

— the one with the power."

I cast a sidelong glance at Edward, but he was gazing into the fire, sipping his tea, his expression blank.

Robert took another chair and arranged himself in it in a studied way, stretching his long legs. I swallowed a sigh. Who did the man seek to impress here? Surely not Cousin Julia. But that left only me.

I put Robert's behavior down to the perennial habits of the predatory male and dismissed him from my mind. For the moment at least.

But Uncle Phillip and Cousin Julia were not so easily dismissed. I was thankful that the boys were still young, and consequently relegated to the nursery, because certainly these relatives of Edward's were not the best of examples. Exciting as they might appear to young minds, stories of ghosts and of summoning Lucifer were hardly the proper background in which to raise healthy children!

Incongruous as this assembly was, though, it was still difficult for me to believe that one of them had killed the old earl, actually taken a human life. And now that person was sitting there among us, as though nothing untoward had ever happened.

It was too difficult to think about and I let my mind slip away to the other subject that frequently filled it — the child I so badly wanted. There was still no sign of its conception and I didn't know whether to be sorry or glad. I wanted our child — I had ceased some time before to think of it as *mine* — but my suspicions of Edward had made me wonder if it was wise to have a child at this time. However, since Edward came often to my bed, and besotted as I was I could not refuse him, the matter seemed clearly out of my hands.

Edward put down his cup and got abruptly to his feet, startling Uncle Phillip and causing Cousin Julia to choke over her fifth tea cake. Edward turned to his brother, his expression so harsh I caught my breath in fear. "Come with me," he said brusquely to Robert. "We have matters to discuss."

Chapter Fourteen

Though we supposed it to be about his allowance, the rest of us did not learn what Edward discussed with Robert that fateful afternoon. No doubt Cousin Julia would not have been above listening at the door, but since I kept both her and Cousin Phillip engaged in conversation, she could not slip away to do so.

When Edward and I retired that evening, I did think about asking him if Robert had been causing more trouble. But my husband seemed moody and withdrawn and I did not want to risk another reprimand such as I had received that morning.

I had thought myself quite a strong woman, self-reliant and above womanish fears, but Edward's anger frightened me. I had no wish to evoke it, most particularly I had no wish to have it directed at me.

So I undressed silently, pulling on my nightdress with fingers that wanted to tremble. I climbed into the big bed and lay shivering. What would Edward do? He usually slept in my chamber, spending the entire night there whether he made love to me or not.

Sometimes, on the nights when he was silent and withdrawn, he did not reach for me, but just lay on his side of the huge bed. Sometimes, then, I swallowed my pride and inched close, close enough to feel the heat of his body. There was a kind of comfort for me in his physical closeness, even if he did not hold me.

But that night when I had about despaired of him touching me, he suddenly gathered me close. A sigh of relief shivered through me.

"Are you cold?" he asked.

"No, no. I am fine." And it was true. When Edward held me, I *was* fine.

"So how has Ned been behaving?" Edward asked.

"Well," I said. "He's been doing well." I schooled myself to calmness, reminding myself of my reasons for deceiving my husband, for not telling him what the boys had found. "I believe the dog is a good influence on him."

Edward sighed. "He's very fond of it." He paused, his hand settling familiarly on the curve of my waist. "And the twins? How are they?"

I knew it cost him effort to talk about his brother's bastard sons. Robert was a real thorn in his side.

"They are well-behaved boys," I said, picking my words carefully. "And they are doing their best to fit in." I sighed. "But Ned does not fully accept them. He treats them more like servants than like friends."

Edward sighed. "That's how it has to be, I suppose. After all, he is going to be the next earl. That separates him from ordinary people."

"Everyone needs friends!" The words burst from me before I could stop them. "Ned is already surrounded by servants." Expecting at any moment to have Edward pull away from me, I hastened to explain more calmly. "He's not an earl yet, you know. He's a lonely little boy, and he desperately needs friends."

"He has you." Edward's voice was strangely husky.

"I am his mother," I replied. "There's a difference."

"Yes," Edward said slowly, as though he were considering each word. "There's a vast difference."

His hand moved upward, came to rest on my breast. "Speaking of mothers," he went on, his voice a throaty whisper. "Shall we see if we can provide you with yet another child to mother?"

I was not deceived by the gentle sarcasm

of his words. Edward was no longer bothered by my desire for his child. In fact, he seemed to share it.

I turned into his arms, my lips close to his. "Yes," I whispered. "Yes."

And in the passionate moments that followed I gave no thought whatsoever to any misgivings about bringing another child into the world, or to my suspicions of its father.

The days wore on, following each other in orderly progression. And my love for Edward continued to grow. I basked in it and tried to put thoughts of the previous earl and his strange death completely out of my mind.

A week passed, a happy, almost ordinary week. And early one afternoon I retired to the closed courtyard garden for a walk. After the mishap on the moor and the shot I thought had been fired at me on the cliff, I was uneasy going alone outside the castle walls. Yet I felt the need for occasional exercise and fresh air.

And so I had begun to frequent the courtyard, a garden formed by the four sides of the castle. It was a relatively large area, bordered with beds of flowers.

Of course they were all withered and

dead, the first frost having killed them. Still, the air was fresh and the sun could be felt, at least in the early afternoon. And so I went daily for a little stroll, a little time to myself.

I took care to inform Hillyer first. Edward's anguish the day he couldn't find me had stuck in my mind. I hadn't dared ask what he'd feared that day, but I knew he feared something.

At any rate, on this particular day I was feeling rather well, congratulating myself that the week had gone smoothly. Perhaps I had exaggerated the things that had happened, I told myself as I took another turn about the garden. Cousin Julia's incessant references to the spirits of the dead had unnerved me. Coincidences *were* possible, I told myself, trying to believe, *wanting* to believe. And I actually had no evidence that I'd been shot at — only that brief sound.

So I paced, round and round the courtyard, almost talking myself into a better, more optimistic frame of mind. The high castle walls kept out the wind. The sun was warm, its cheerful heat raised my spirits, helped me think only of the best things.

Finally I smiled and set myself to imagining how I should have the flower beds planted come spring. Over there I would have a great bed of wildflowers brought in from the moor. And in that corner — a corner that seemed particularly dark because the sun had moved and the walls now threw it into gloom — in that corner I would have the gardener plant a bed of bright marigolds.

Their brilliance would brighten the entire courtyard. I paused for a moment, turning my back to the shadows by the wall, and contemplated the entire courtyard. It was sadly overgrown by tall ragged weeds, but come spring I would make of it a —

A sound behind me made me start. I whirled, thinking to catch the boys creeping up to play a trick on me. But before I could see anything, I felt a terrible sharp pain on the back of my head and the world exploded into a blackness laced with stars.

I don't know how long I lay unconscious. I remember a vague feeling of unrest as I slowly struggled toward consciousness. My head was throbbing with the most dreadful pain and my elbow felt wrenched.

I lay still, trying to make some sense out of my hazy recollection. There had been the noise. I remembered that.

Had I turned too quickly, tripped and fallen, hitting my head in the process? Yet I distinctly remembered feeling the pain *before* I fell. And what was that strange odor, that rustling noise, that prickling sensation against my head and cheek.

Slowly I opened my eyes.

And then the horror of it hit me! It was hay I smelled, straw I felt against my cheek. And the dark shape that loomed over me was a horse! The big black stallion that Edward had recently purchased, the horse that I believed had tried to trample me on the moor!

I shrank back against the floor, choking down the scream that burbled in my throat. A horse! This was no accident. Someone had brought me here, had left me at the mercy of this great brute. Someone who knew — I could not think about that now.

I cowered against the stable wall, my limbs gone into a wild trembling. The stallion, smelling my fear, shifted uneasily, whinnying deep in his throat.

My mind raced, my thoughts in chaos. "No," I moaned. If I could have, I would have clawed my way out through the stable wall, but of course I could not. I could only crouch there, trying to think, trying not to scream.

The horse snorted and danced sideways, tossing his dark mane. Another, even worse, fit of trembling overtook me.

I tried to think. Think! I told myself
sternly. I wrapped my arms around myself
to still my quaking. And suddenly, in the
back of my mind, I could hear Ned's voice.
"Horses don't hurt you on purpose," he was
saying. "The thing is they get afraid too.
You have to move slowly. And talk to them.
So they know you like them."

Slowly, slowly, I repeated to myself. *They
get afraid too.*

The horse danced again, his hooves
moving closer, striking the straw near my
skirt with sharp, deadly blows.

"Easy, easy," I said. "Easy, boy." *Slowly,
move slowly.*

My back to the wall, my eyes on the huge
animal before me, I pushed myself slowly
erect. Inch by quivering inch, I pushed
myself up. The wall behind me was rough.
Splinters caught at my cloak, gouged my
trembling fingers, but I persisted, slowly
bringing myself upright.

"Nice boy," I crooned. "You're a beauty.
Such a beauty. I won't hurt you. Easy, easy
now."

Finally I stood erect, my knees barely
keeping me upright. Carefully, step by step,
I edged toward the stall door. The stallion
snorted again, moving closer to me. I froze.

He was huge, a tremendous animal whose bulk stood between me and safety.

I took another breath, swallowing the scream that wanted to rip from my throat. The horse moved closer still.

I pressed back against the wall, my breath catching in my throat. And the stallion thrust his great head toward me. In the gloom I could see him bare his huge teeth. They came closer and closer.

And then, just before my knees gave way and I slid to the floor, the beast brushed my cheek with his nose. I gasped, thinking he meant to hurt me. And then he nuzzled me, slowly and carefully.

The animal meant its overtures to be friendly. It liked me!

I reached a tentative hand to stroke the big head feeling the silken hair, the warm rippling muscle. There was a comfort to the feel of the horse, a warmth under my fingers I had never imagined.

The horse whuffled, shaking his head slightly, nosing against my shoulder. Laughter bubbled out of me — half-hysterical laughter it was true, but laughter nevertheless. Still laughing, I threw my arms around the horse's neck and buried my face in his sweet-smelling mane.

"Bless you, Ned," I murmured. "Oh bless

you." The boy — and his advice — had probably saved my life. I stroked the great horse's muscled neck. "Such a beauty you are," I whispered. "Such a marvelous beauty."

I stroked the horse for a while longer, then made my way to the door and eased out of the stall. My mysterious assailant had failed again. His effort to frighten me had, instead, cured me of my fear of horses.

I brushed the straw from my clothing and turned toward the house. I wished that I could forget this latest attack on my person, but I could not. There was no possible way that this could have been an accident.

Though I might have fallen, I could not possibly have gotten into the stable by myself. Someone had carried me there, someone who knew about my fear of horses. But no one knew about that — only Ned.

I stopped on the darkening pathway to the castle, almost overcome by the terrible wave of paralyzing nausea that swept over me. Edward knew. That first day Edward had told me I would not be required to ride with Ned. Oh, Edward!

My knees failed me then, and I sank down on the cold stone walk, overcome by my fear. Oh God! Edward, my Edward, knew my fear of horses.

I buried my face in my shaking hands.

Edward *had* been the one to benefit from his father's death. He, after all, had succeeded to the title. But why then had he married me? Why had he brought me to Grey Cliffs, to this godforsaken place? I could see no reason for him complicating his life by taking a wife.

But perhaps there *was* a reason, some reason I could not ascertain. *Oh God*, I prayed. *Help me. Help me know what to do.*

After my prayer, I felt somewhat better. I had no solution to my dilemma, of course, but putting my problems in God's hands had relieved my mind, at least a little.

I got slowly to my feet and prepared to return to the castle. I had made two sacred promises — the one about Ned to his father, and the other — my marriage vows — to God. I could not break either of them.

But even had I been willing to break my vows, I would not have left Edward. My life was inextricably interwoven with my husband's. And I knew, to my dismay, that I would reject anyone or anything that tried to separate me from him.

By the time I reached the castle my head was pounding horribly and my elbow felt bruised to the bone. But that pain was nothing to the pain festering in my heart.

I made my way to the library, determined to present a normal face to the world. Perhaps my reappearance, looking ordinary, would startle the attacker, cause him to give himself away.

I had about decided that my attacker must be male. Someone had transported me from the courtyard to the stable, after all — a considerable distance. Surely Cousin Julia could not have done such a thing, at least not alone. Although I had heard that demented people sometimes were capable of deeds of great and marvelous strength.

I sank down in my chair, holding out my icy hands to the warmth of the flames. As always, the heat barely reached me. The room remained chill and dank. But my heart was even colder.

As I waited for Hillyer to bring the hot tea I'd ordered, I allowed my eyes to close. I was a strong woman, determined in my purpose, but I didn't know how long I could bear up under such strain.

Though I had stopped asking questions, the attacker had not let me be. Someone still believed me a danger — and would continue to believe so until he disposed of me or I found him out.

It seemed I had only one choice — I must find the killer and expose him. But how?

Chapter Fifteen

The next day the weather turned really warm. The sun and the heat made it seem almost like spring outside. Yet the castle remained cold. Gazing out the nursery window, I shivered at the prospect of yet another day in the castle's dark environs. I simply would not do it.

I turned to the boys, occupied with the sums on their slates. "Put down your chalk," I said cheerfully. "Put on your stout walking shoes and warm clothes."

"Where are —"

"We going?" asked the twins.

"Are we going for a walk?" Ned asked glaring at the other two.

"Yes," I replied, ignoring his bad manners. "We're going for an excursion on the moor."

The twins looked at each other and smiled.

"Captain, too?" Ned whistled for the dog.

I nodded. "Of course. We wouldn't leave him at home."

The boys were ready in no time, and, leaving Betty with instructions for ordering up a supper against our return, we set out.

As I watched the boys trudging ahead of me, I mused on the relationships between them. Ned was still the undisputed leader. That didn't bother me so much, but I still didn't care for the way he ordered the twins about, as though they existed merely for his convenience. However, I knew talking would have little effect on him. It would take something else — at the time I didn't know what — to convince the boy that friends were more valuable than servitors.

For some time we made our way through the twisted stunted oaks where the sun barely reached, and then we were on the moor. We had not come out where I had been the afternoon the horseman tried to trample me, but farther toward the sea. The smell of it was strong in my nostrils, the taste of salt on my tongue.

I smiled. I loved the ocean — its beauty and its grandeur. But I knew it could be capricious.

"Stay back from the waves," I instructed. "I don't want you to get wet and take a chill."

The boys nodded and began exploring the shoreline for the kinds of treasures boys are always excited by — a shell, a feather, a piece of weathered wood.

I found a big flat rock and made myself a spot on it — a nice warm comfortable spot — and prepared to spend some soothing hours in the sun.

But I had no sooner removed my bonnet and disposed my skirts nicely around me than the dog yapped excitedly and broke away from the boys, rushing off across the sand at a great pace.

"Captain! Come back!" Ned yelled after him. But to no avail — the dog just kept going.

"He's not gonna come," Peter said.

"He wants that rabbit," Paul added.

Ned was already chasing after the dog, disgust in his voice as he cried, "Captain, stop! Come back here!"

The boy disappeared around a sand dune, then from farther down the beach we heard his scream of terror. "Captain! No! Don't!"

The twins stared at each other with wide eyes, their faces fear-stricken.

"Help!" Ned screamed. "Help!"

The twins set off running. Gathering up my skirts, I scrambled after them, my heart pounding in my throat.

The sand seemed to conspire to impede my progress, to hold me back, but I struggled on. Once I tripped over a snarl of seaweed, falling to the wet sand on my hands and knees. I scrambled to my feet, grabbed up my sodden skirts and ran on.

Finally I came to a halt by a large mound of sand. The twins stood there, jabbering excitedly. I followed their gaze. God, no!

The dog was floundering in a pool of wet sand, sinking in it. And Ned was about to step into it, too!

"Quicksand!" Peter cried, tugging at my wet skirt.

"Stop Ned!" Paul begged.

"Ned! Wait!" My voice was hoarse. I was panting so I could hardly breathe.

But Ned ignored me. In another moment he, too, would be mired in the quicksand. "Stop!" I cried. "Stop!"

"We'll help," Peter yelled. "Lay down."

For a moment I thought the boy's mind had snapped. Paul tugged again at my skirt. "Won't sink so fast," he explained.

Peter hurried off across the sand, picking up a piece of driftwood as he went.

The dog had stopped making any noise. It struggled silently, its eyes on its master. In a few more minutes the sand would close over its shaggy black head.

"Come," Peter said, pulling at me. I followed him toward the others.

Ned lay flat in the wet sand, his agonized gaze on the dog, whose struggles were growing more feeble.

The twins dropped to the sand, inching forward. Peter pushed the driftwood before him. After what seemed like an eternity, he reached Ned.

"Captain!" the boy cried. "Please! Help him."

"I'll get him," Peter said, inching forward again.

"He's mine," Ned cried, trying to follow.

Paul pulled him back down. "Peter knows how. He saved our dog."

"But Captain's mine," Ned cried. "I should —"

"Too many make the wood sink," Paul insisted, holding tight to Ned's jacket.

I watched, hardly daring to breathe while the boy inched slowly forward. The dog had ceased to struggle. Nothing but the tip of his muzzle remained above the surface.

Dear God, I prayed. *Save the boy's dog. Let Peter get there in time.*

Paul turned to Ned. "I have to follow Peter. You follow me. When I call, hold my ankles."

Ned nodded. "I will."

Peter was stretched across the quicksand, his feet at the very edge. Paul crept forward behind his brother. A chain! They meant to form a human chain to pull the dog to safety. *Oh God, help them.*

Finally, after what seemed like hours, Peter reached the dog. "It's all right now," he said to the exhausted animal. Slowly and carefully, he worked the piece of wood under Captain, using it almost like a lever to break the suction of the sand.

Then he wrapped his arms around the animal, keeping its head on his shoulder. "Now," he cried. "Pull, but easy."

Paul took ahold of Peter's ankles and Ned took Paul's. Hastily I knelt and held Ned's. Slowly and carefully, our hearts in our throats, we eased backward across the wet sand, an inch at a time, until finally, triumphantly, Peter and the dog were safe on solid ground.

Ned scrambled over to them, tears running down his cheeks. "Captain! Oh Captain! You stupid dog!" He clasped the filthy animal in his arms.

Then, with a look that brought tears to my eyes, he turned to Peter. "He would have died. You saved him." He put a grimy arm around Peter's shoulders.

"We all saved him," Peter said.

"Couldn't anyone do it alone," Paul added.

The dog yipped weakly and licked Ned's face.

"I — Thank you," Ned mumbled.

His face told me that at last Ned had friends he valued. I turned away for a moment, dashing the tears from my eyes. "Well," I said when I turned back. "What an excursion this has been!"

The boys looked up from the dog, their eyes wide, their dirty faces split with grins.

"I think we should get back to the castle and clean up," I told them. "We'll have another outing soon."

Ned looked down at the dog in his arms. "Maybe we'll leave Captain at home."

Peter laughed. "I bet he won't chase any rabbits."

Paul laughed too. "For a long time."

For a moment I thought Ned would revert to his old behavior, but then he grinned. "If he starts chasing anything, we'll have to teach him different. We don't want to be fishing our dog out of quicksand all the time."

I saw the glance the twins exchanged, a look of almost pure joy. My own face must have been glowing with happiness. One of my prayers had been answered: Ned had found the friends he so badly needed. And the twins had found acceptance.

My hands tightened in the folds of my clammy skirt. Would my other prayers be answered? Would I one day hold my own child? I shivered, but not because my clothes were wet. *Would* I have a child of my own — or would my search for the old earl's murderer bring death and disaster to us all?

We reached the castle, a wet and bedraggled but thoroughly joyful little band. Up the great stairs we traipsed, past Hillyer's disapproving stare, dripping sand and water behind us.

When we reached the nursery, Betty raised a shocked hand to her lips. "Lord have mercy! You look like a bunch of drowned ghosts!"

She bustled about, ringing for hot water and towels. I left the boys, happily preparing to bathe, dog and all, and repaired to my room.

This latest misadventure, harrowing as it had been, had not lowered my spirits. It could not be laid at anyone's door, and it certainly had had a favorable outcome.

I stepped out of my sodden gown, preparing to wash off the grime of our adventure.

And then the hair on the back of my neck began to rise. Someone was watching me!

I turned, but the door to the hall was closed just as I had left it. A shiver raced over me. Who was watching me? And how?

A sound to my right made me whirl — and then relief washed over me. "Edward! How long have you been standing there?"

"Not long," he said, his eyes gone dark.

My heart throbbed in my throat, my hands went clammy. Had it been Edward's gaze I felt?

He crossed to my side. "Your excursion was rather a wet one," he said with a smile, running a finger across my bare shoulder.

As always my body responded to his touch. "Yes," I whispered, turning my face to his.

For a long moment he looked down into my eyes, his own so heated I felt almost scorched. And then without another word, he swung me up into his arms, wet underclothes and all, and carried me to the great bed.

Later, snug against his warm body, I told him what had transpired on the beach. His body stiffened and he clutched me tighter, but he did not grow angry. In fact, I thought I detected pride in his voice when he said, "They're good boys, the twins."

I snuggled against him, relishing this moment of emotional closeness. "It's good you gave them a home," I commented.

Edward actually chuckled. "Are you

trying to tell me that I have been repaid for doing a good deed?"

"Perhaps," I said. "Who's to say for sure?"

"Who indeed?" he replied, pulling me into another embrace.

We were none of us the worse for our contention with the quicksand. Thanks to Betty's efficiency, everyone, including the dog, was bathed and cossetted, fed hot milk and cakes, and quickly recovered.

It had been frightening, but I was sure Ned had learned from the experience. And since I had forbidden him to go alone on the moor and he had emphatically agreed not to do so, I felt fairly safe on that score.

For a few days the excitement of that afternoon drove most other thoughts from my mind. But as the boys suffered no ill effects and life at Grey Cliffs returned to what passed for normal, thoughts of the old earl began again to intrude into my consciousness. I did not want to think about the old man's death. By all accounts he had been an autocratic tyrant, feared and disliked by everyone except Robert, the son who was so like him. Certainly Edward and Uncle Phillip had little good to say of him. But whatever my feelings of disgust for the old man, he had been a human being. No one had the right to kill another human being.

But it certainly seemed that someone *had* killed him. Else why had the attacks been made on me?

The boys wanted me to explore the secret passageways with them, but some second sense, some premonition, kept me from assenting. However, since I did not like the idea of them being in the passageways alone, I instructed Betty to stay with them whenever they left the nursery. I knew they would not risk her knowing their secret.

The weather remained pleasant for a week after our excursion to the beach, and the boys, now real friends and companions, took to playing in the courtyard garden. I didn't fear their being there — all the attacks had been made on me. The children knew nothing and the attacker was aware of that.

Edward continued to be pleasant to me. Sometimes my conscience pricked me at the thought that I was deceiving him, that I had not told him about the boys' discovery of the passageway. But things had been so pleasant between us. His spells of moodiness and withdrawal seemed briefer, his tenderness with me more pronounced. I hesitated to spoil the good feeling that existed between us.

And so I went on, trying to ignore the danger that stalked me, trying desperately to find some other explanations for the so-called "accidents." I still had not told Edward about the pistol shot. Nor about waking up in the great stallion's stall.

That was what frightened me the most in those dark moments before dawn when I lay, wide-eyed and terrified, unable to sleep. Not the memory of being in the stall, for thanks to Ned I was no longer afraid of horses. My fright came because only two people living knew of my feeling about horses. And one of them was a boy, too young and too small to have dragged me to the stable, even supposing that he had been able to knock me out.

But Edward — Edward who'd learned of my fear from Jeremy. Edward who touched me so tenderly, held me so closely —

When I got that far in my nightly examinations, I could go no further. I rolled toward the husband sleeping beside me. Close against his warm back, I refused to think ill of him. And finally I slept.

Such disregard of the facts was foolish, but I was a young woman, newly in love. And I was besotted with my husband, waiting for his smile, his touch, like any green schoolroom girl waits for the man of her dreams. In some way I knew that, but I was powerless to change it.

And so things continued. Perhaps they would have gone on that way indefinitely, but then the dog dug up the box.

Chapter Sixteen

About a week after our excursion, Ned and the twins came hurrying into the nursery. "Look, Hester!" Ned cried. "Captain dug this up!"

He extended a tin box, dented and dirty.

"He kept whining," Peter said.

"We were playing in the courtyard," Paul added.

Ned waved the box. "And then he dug this up. What do you think's in it?" he asked, handing it to me.

"I don't know." I looked down at the box. It wasn't heavy. How had the dog known to find it? My heart skipped a beat. Had it belonged to the old earl?

Ned pressed closer. "We didn't open it," he said. "We brought it right to you."

I smiled at them. "That was very wise. I doubt that it's something important, though. People seldom bury important things in the garden."

Ned's face fell. "We thought it might be buried treasure."

I smiled at the childish wish, but I could not keep my mind from racing. People *did* on occasion bury important things. Could the old earl have left some information, something to lead to his killer?

I tried the box but it would not open.

"Needs a key," Peter said.

"Or something to break the lock," Paul contributed.

Betty, who had trailed in after the boys, grinned. "I hear tell a hairpin's most as good as a key for opening locks."

I hesitated, but the temptation was strong. I might be holding the answer to everything right there in my hands. "Well—"

Betty pulled a hairpin from her tumbled hair and offered it to me. The boys waited, faces filled with excitement. I could not help myself. I took the hairpin from Betty's outstretched hand.

It took but a few moments, wiggling the pin a little, and the lid of the box sprang open. The boys moved at the same instant, jostling each other as they peered eagerly into the box.

"Papers," Peter said in disgust.

"Just papers," Paul echoed.

"No treasure?" Ned said. "I thought there'd be treasure."

"It's just an old box," I said. "Perhaps your father buried it when he was a boy."

I kept my expression calm, my voice even.

The boys must not guess the excitement I was feeling.

"Can we have it?" Ned asked.

I hesitated only a moment. "Of course. I'll just take the papers." I lifted them out, some faded letters.

The boys took the box and went off to a corner, where they began making up stories of buried boxes full of treasure.

With a glance at Betty, I set off for my chamber. Once there I locked the door and sank trembling into a chair.

My fingers shook as I eased the first letter open. It was so old the ink had faded, but I could still make the writing out.

The letter was addressed to the old earl and was — I soon discovered — a love letter. Evidently it was written by a young woman, someone the earl had once possessed. She wrote with such longing of their times together, of the joy of her love for him and her pain when she could no longer be with him. Tears filled my eyes as I read about this young woman's shattering hurt when the man no longer wanted her.

I blinked and turned to the last page. And blinked again. Julia. The signature said Julia!

Hurriedly I took out the other letters. They were all the same — protestations of love for the man, pleas to be taken back into his affections. And evidently all to no avail.

I leaned back in my chair. I didn't know which seemed more difficult to believe — that Cousin Julia had once been young and beautiful, or that she had allowed herself to be taken advantage of by the earl, who even in his youth must have been quite the roué.

I sat for some time, staring at the faded letters, musing over the vagaries of love, before it occurred to me that these letters presented the perfect motive for murder. He had used Cousin Julia dreadfully and then abandoned her. Could this have turned her mind, finally deranged her, so that she took her revenge by killing him?

The thought was appalling. Cousin Julia a murderer! My mind simply would not accept it. Motive she might — and did — have. And opportunity. But she didn't have the means. The old earl had been a big man, as big as Edward by all reports. And Cousin Julia was a short woman, much too heavy for her height. To imagine her hoisting the earl's body so as to hang it from the chandelier — I just couldn't do it. I might as well imagine spindly Uncle Phillip doing such a thing. It just wouldn't wash.

I got up and tucked the letters away, slipping them atop the canopy of the bed where no one was likely to look until cleaning time. And then I tried to put the whole thing out of my mind.

Still, later that evening when we gathered for dinner, I found myself looking at Cousin Julia through different eyes. She had once been young and beautiful, she had once been caught in the throes of passion. Wrongful passion, of course, but passion nevertheless. I felt a certain kinship to her, a certain sense of her humanity that I had not felt before.

The next afternoon Edward visited the nursery, one of his periodic visits that never occurred at prearranged times. The boys looked up when he came in. The twins bobbed their heads and remained silent, but Ned jumped up and went to his father. "Papa, it's good to see you," the boy said with a formality that nearly broke my heart.

Edward nodded. To my dismay the two didn't even touch each other.

"How are your lessons going?" Edward asked.

"Very well, Papa. Hester says I'm learning just as I should."

Edward smiled. "That's good. Hester know."

During this exchange the twins had remained silent, bent over their slates. Now they raised their heads and exchanged glances. I swallowed. Would Edward speak to the twins or would he ignore them?

I looked at them, their golden heads bent again, their faces wrinkled in concentration as they traced the letters I had given them.

And Edward turned. "Peter, Paul," he said. I warmed to the kindness in his tone. "I heard what a fine thing you did, helping Ned save the dog."

The twins looked up, their faces wreathed in smiles, their eyes shining. "Thank you, Your Lordship," they said in unison.

A shadow crossed Edward's face. "Call me Uncle Edward," he said slowly, his gaze moving to me.

The twins appeared as surprised as I was, but they hastened to say, "Yes, Uncle Edward."

Peter hesitated, then took a deep breath and went on. "Milord, Uncle Edward, could — would —" The boy stopped, plainly nervous.

"What is it, Peter?"

I controlled my elation. If Edward could tell the twins apart, he had been paying them much more mind than I thought. A little prickle of fear followed the elation.

Did he know the boys had found the passageway?

But he couldn't, I told myself firmly. If he knew that, he would surely have remonstrated with me.

Peter moistened his lips, sent me a pleading glance, and stumbled on. "It's our — our father, mi— Uncle Edward. We'd like —" Peter looked to Paul, who nodded eagerly. "We'd like to have him stay here all the time."

To my surprise Edward did not frown. His face took on a wistful, boyish look. "I'd like that, too," he said. "When we were young, we used to be great friends." He sighed and shook himself. "But your father's a grown man. I can't keep him here."

The twins nodded and bent again to their slates. Edward sent me a pained look "But I will talk to him about it."

"Thank you!" The words burst from the twins in unison and they ran to throw themselves onto Edward and give him a great hug. Ned sent me an astonished look and then, not to be undone, hurried to join them.

Looking at my husband, at the happy children gathered around him, I had a momentary vision of a little face — a dark little face topped with black curls, a little girl face. I hugged the vision to me, the vision of *our* child, and smiled.

The next few mornings I was unaccountably ill. I hoped that my queasiness might be caused by my being with child, but it was too soon to know with certainty.

I kept alert, not going to the courtyard or anywhere else alone. But nothing unusual happened. The boys had become great friends and I was heartened by their camaraderie. But I was so torn over my feelings about Edward that I could not really enjoy the boys' triumph.

Several nights later, I lay in bed awake. Over and over, I examined every single piece of information I had about the old earl, about his mysterious death, about the people who might have caused it.

Robert was hasty, a man given to quick forbidden pleasures, but I could not imagine him taking his father's life in that premeditated way. A quick blow in anger, perhaps, but not this calculated pseudo-suicide. There was no reason for it.

Cousin Julia had good reason. The passion of her letters still lingered in my mind. But all my original reservations concerning her remained, too. The physical aspects of the act still seemed beyond her. Unless she had someone to help her.

There was Uncle Phillip, of course, though I couldn't imagine the two of them ever working together. I even looked closely at Uncle Phillip's possible motives. But what had the old bumbler to gain? The earl's death had brought the title to Edward. If he died — I shivered — the title would go to Ned. Should something happen to Ned — God forbid — the earldom would be Robert's. Uncle Phillip was a little strange, and why anyone should *want* to summon the devil was incomprehensible to me. But to imagine that bumbling old man had planned a murder — it was just too much.

And that brought me back to the one person who was left — Edward. The man slept peacefully beside me, his thigh pressed against mine. I wanted my mind to stop its mad racing, to refute my suspicions of the man I loved, but everything seemed to point in his direction. *He* became the new earl. *He* had hated his father. He was out of the castle when the horseman tried to run me down, when the shot whistled past my ear. And most damning of all — he knew my fear of horses.

Edward stirred in his sleep, throwing an arm over me. And deep inside me I thought

I felt the stirs of new life. Great tears coursed down my cheeks. Was the child I hoped I carried begotten by a murderer?

I slept, finally, exhausted by the turmoil of my thoughts. When I woke the room was dark — and I knew instantly that something was wrong. Automatically I felt for Edward, but the bed beside me was cold. Edward was gone.

My seeking fingers encountered a piece of paper. Holding tightly to it, I groped for the candle and struck the flint. I held the candle close to the note, trying to make out the letters.

The script was bold and black. I did not recognize the hand. But the words sent terror to my heart.

"I want the letters," the note read. "Bring them to the priest hole tonight. Or tomorrow you will be a widow."

My hand shook so that I could scarcely see to tell if that was all to the message. But it was. There was no signature, nothing more.

An icy chill crept over me. Edward. Where was Edward?

The note quivered in my hand. A widow, it said. That meant the writer had Edward.

But how? How could anyone take my husband from beside me while I lay sleeping? Surely I would have heard them.

I could not let anything happen to Edward. And yet — Edward was the only one who knew my fear of horses. Edward had supposedly been gone when the attacks on me had occurred. And — most damaging in my mind — Edward had made light of my concerns and suspicions over his father's death.

But why should *he* wish to lure me from my bed? Any night he could have disposed of me as I slept — helpless — beside him. My heart beat faster. I had just realized what anyone must. A wife found dead in her bed must cast suspicion on a husband. But one who has wandered off, gotten immured in an ancient priest hole — I trembled so that the note fell from my fingers.

Then I forced myself to think. If the murderer was not Edward, and I did not take the letters to him, my husband would die. And if the villain actually was Edward, *I* would die. I stared Death in the eye, there in my cold bed, and I found Him not so terrible. Dying could be no worse than living without Edward.

And so I rose, pulled on my dressing gown and slippers, and retrieved the letters from the canopy, tucking them into the pocket of my robe.

Chapter Seventeen

Lighting a fresh candle, I set out for the gallery. But as I neared the nursery I was overcome with tenderness and a desire to see the children one last time. So I crept in to have a quick peek. They slept, their faces angelic. I kissed each smooth forehead, and over Ned I whispered a little prayer that morning might find him still with two living parents.

Then, clutching my candle, I made my way to the portrait gallery. The hall was black and my candle's light feeble, but still I kept going. Edward was my life. One way or another, I must be with him.

The candle flickered, its glow so pale in the darkness. I reached the portrait, pulled it aside. The passageway was black as the nether regions, but I had no choice. I swallowed and stepped in.

The passageway was dark as pitch. I inched along, one hand holding the candle high, the other clutching the letters I had put in the pocket of my dressing gown.

Finally, after what seemed like ages, I reached the priest hole. Slowly, my heart in my throat, I pushed open the door. More darkness greeted me. I took a step, peering around me. The dark little room seemed empty. My heart threatened to choke me. Then I heard a groan from the far corner.

Clutching my candle, I hurried across the room. And almost swooned.

Edward lay in the corner, his eyes closed, a red stain on his forehead. Fear brought me to my knees beside him, but it was fear mingled with blessed relief. Edward could not have done this to himself. Edward was innocent!

Quickly I tried to ascertain the nature of his injuries, but the wound on his head was all I could find. As I knelt, bent over him, he opened his eyes. "Hester! Go! Leave me!"

But I could not leave him. My beloved husband. "Let me help —"

Across the room the door thudded shut. The draft from its closing blew out my candle. In the utter darkness I clutched my husband's arm.

"Too late." He groaned, struggling to his feet and pulling me up with him. "Too —"

The door creaked slowly open again. That crazy laughter echoed through the room. "Five minutes." The words sent a chill down my spine. "You have five minutes to make your good-byes."

Uncle Phillip stood in the doorway, the

light from his candle revealing the madness in his eyes, the pistol in his hand. He stepped in, letting the door swing shut behind him.

"Too bad," he said. "I've no complaint against you, Hester. I tried to warn you away."

"Yes," I said, willing myself to remain calm. "I know you did. But why should you wish to hurt Edward? He has given you a home and —"

Uncle Phillip laughed, the laughter of insanity. "Oh yes, he gave me a home. Just like my brother before him. My dear brother!" His face twisted in rage. "Always laughing at me. But I fixed him." He nodded slowly. "Oh yes. I laced his pudding, his anise pudding, with laudanum. And then, while he slept, I hung him."

The man meant to kill us. It was plain in his eyes, his mad eyes. I faltered, but Edward's arm around me sustained me.

"It was easy," Uncle Phillip went on, his eyes gleaming. "No one suspected *me*." He laughed again. "All my life people have laughed at me, called me a bumbler." He cackled, shuffling his feet in the old carpet slippers. "I let them. No one suspects a bumbler, you see."

He waved the pistol. "With you two gone,

Robert and Ned will have accidents and *I'll* be the earl."

My heart rose up in my throat. Ned! "You would kill a boy?" I asked, my voice incredulous.

Uncle Phillip shrugged. "I mean to be earl."

"It's no use," Edward said. "I've tried to reason with him." The arm he had around me tightened. "Hester, my love. I should never have brought you here." He sighed. "I thought you would be safe."

I turned my face to his. "Edward. Don't blame yourself. I love you and —"

Uncle Phillip snorted. "Very nice." He looked at me. "Where are Julia's letters?"

"How did you know about them?"

He chuckled, a sound even more frightening than his laughter. "I watched you. The passageway has peepholes into the rooms. I saw you read the letters. But I couldn't see where you put them."

He frowned. "My greedy brother took her, too. Julia was a lovely young thing then, fresh, beautiful. He used her and threw her aside. But she went on loving him, wouldn't have anything to do with me."

Even in my fear, I felt pity for him. Poor man. He had obviously loved Julia very much.

My mind raced, trying to think of something, some way to save us. In the meantime, I must keep him talking. "Uncle Phillip, it was you! You were the ghost!"

"Of course." He nodded craftily, his pistol never wavering. "Made a good one, too, didn't I? Had all the servants on pins and needles."

"That was you laughing in the passageway the other day."

He smiled, punctuating each sentence with a nod. "Yes, that was me. And it was me on Edward's new horse. And me who shot at you on the cliff. And me who knocked you on the head and left you in the stallion's stall."

Edward's arm tightened around me as the recital continued.

"But you wouldn't take the hint," Uncle Phillip complained. "You wouldn't leave."

"I couldn't," I said simply. "I love Edward. And I love the children."

"Too bad," Uncle Phillip repeated. "You have to die too. Robert's boys, they're all right. But Ned has to go."

I could feel Edward tensing at the thought of Ned in jeopardy. I tightened my hold on my husband's arm. The room was small. At such a short distance Uncle Phillip wasn't likely to miss.

And then to my complete astonishment I saw a thin line of light appear under the door. Since Uncle Phillip stood with his back to it, he didn't see the light, but Edward saw it. I felt the slow relaxation of the muscles in the arm my fingers clutched.

Thank God! We were not facing this madman alone. Someone was on the other side of that door!

"I cannot believe that you would kill a child," I said. "Have you no fear of divine retribution?"

Uncle Phillip laughed. "There is no God," he said. "No devil either. I should know, I've tried to call him up enough times. And with what I've done, he should answer me."

"But the ghost," I went on. "Aren't you afraid of your brother's ghost?"

"There aren't any ghosts either."

"Then that was you I heard in the oak grove the other day," I said. "And you I saw in the portrait gallery last Tuesday." And I went on to name many days and places where I had seen the ghost. Of course I had not seen him or anything else — but Uncle Phillip couldn't know that.

Every time, he nodded, signifying that he had indeed been the one I'd seen. But in the feeble light of the candle his face was growing even paler. I knew I was reaching him, frightening him, but would it be enough? And who was outside the door? Why didn't they come to our help?

"I still should think you'd be afraid," I cried. "If *I* murdered someone, *I* would be afraid."

"I told you," he said with a mad kind of patience. "There are no ghosts. No one will suspect me."

And the next moment, from outside the door, came the most horrifying moan. Then a ghostly voice wailed, "Phil-lip. Why?"

Uncle Phillip paled still further, but the pistol remained pointed at us. Beside me, Edward seemed to be holding his breath.

Please God, I prayed silently. *Help us.*

Another moan sounded from outside the door. Uncle Phillip groaned and whirled, throwing it open. A white shape loomed in the darkness there.

Edward hurtled past me, throwing himself at Uncle Phillip's back. The pistol went clattering across the room to land against the wall. On hands and knees I scrambled to grab it.

Edward hauled Uncle Phillip to his feet. Without his pistol, the little man looked dazed, almost pitiful. To think that he had killed his brother — and had meant to kill us!

The ghostly shape spoke. "Hester, are you all right?"

"Ned? Ned, is that you?"

I stared as the sheet fell away, revealing Ned perched on Paul's shoulders.

"Yes," Ned cried, jumping down. "It's me." He ran to hug me and Paul followed.

"What are you doing here?" I asked, giving the pistol to Edward and gathering them close.

"I got so scared," Ned said, squeezing me even tighter. "I heard you praying and I knew something was wrong. So I woke up the twins."

I swallowed. That little prayer over Ned had very likely saved our lives.

"We hurried and followed you," Ned went on. "We saw you go in the passageway."

Paul nodded. "But just when we were going to follow, Uncle Phillip came along."

"So Peter went for his father," Ned went on. "And Paul and I came after you. We heard what you were saying and so we decided to try to scare him."

Edward chuckled. "You certainly did that. You're some brave boys."

"But the sheet —" I began.

Ned looked down at the floor, his expression sheepish. "We — we had it in the passageway, Hester. Sometimes —" He looked to Paul.

Paul took a deep breath and looked me in the eye. "Sometimes we used it to scare the servants."

"But we won't anymore," Ned promised with a look to his father. "Not ever."

"I should hope not," Edward said, and I thought I detected a note of laughter in his voice.

"Paul? Ned?" Robert's voice came echoing down the passageway. "Where are you?"

"In here, Papa," Paul called, his face alight.

Robert came barreling in, Peter at his heels. To my complete surprise Edward's brother fell to his knees and clasped his son to him. "Paul! Thank God you're all right. And Ned?"

"I'm fine, Uncle Robert." Ned's face glowed with boyish pride. "We made a ghost. And we saved Papa and Hes— And Mama."

My heart swelled up in my throat. Ned had called me Mama.

But Robert didn't notice. He got to his feet and looked to Edward in confusion. "What happened here? What's wrong with Uncle Phillip? And why the pistol?"

Edward sighed. "It's a long story, but the

upshot of it is that Uncle Phillip killed our father."

"Killed?" Robert repeated, stunned.

"Yes," Edward said. "Fed him anise pudding laced with laudanum and then arranged the suicide."

"It's mine," Uncle Phillip murmured. "Everything is mine. You can't have it."

"He meant to kill us," Edward went on. "Then arrange accidents for Ned and you, and eventually he would become the earl."

Peter ran to hug his father. "It's all right, Papa. He won't hurt you now."

Nodding, Robert pulled him closer. In his disheveled nightclothes, with his arms around his sons, Robert looked more the man than I had ever seen him.

He took the pistol from Edward. "I'll take Uncle Phillip. You'd better attend to Hester. She's not looking very well. Boys, you come with me."

Robert led Uncle Phillip out and the boys followed, leaving us with a single candle on the table. Edward took me in his arms. "Oh, Hester, to think I almost lost you!"

Close against his chest I gave silent thanksgiving for our rescue. And for the knowledge that my husband had had nothing to do with his father's death or the attacks on me.

"Dear God, Hester," Edward was saying. "I love you so much. But it was wrong of me to bring you here. I suspected, nay, I feared, foul play in my father's death. But I never thought *you* would be in danger."

"You married me so Ned would have someone to care for him," I said. "Because you feared for your own life."

He nodded. "Yes, but I didn't dare tell you. At first because I needed you so badly for the boy's sake — and later because I knew you loved me. And if you thought I was in danger you would certainly persist in your efforts to find my father's killer. And put yourself in more danger. I couldn't stand that."

I raised my face for his kiss. Afterward he said, "But why didn't you tell me about these other attacks on you?"

I didn't know what to say and so I remained silent.

He waited, then his face went pale. "Hester, you suspected me!"

I could not deny it. I wanted no more deception between us. "Sometimes," I admitted. "But always I loved you. And when I woke and found the note, I had to come, to try to save you."

He hugged me close. "My darling. At last we can lead a normal life. Wait, Hester, what letters was he talking about?"

"The dog dug up a box in the garden. It contained letters to your father, from Cousin Julia when she was young. She — ah — apparently —"

"They were lovers," Edward said. "And then he discarded her. I suspected as much. Uncle Phillip no doubt meant to use the letters to cast suspicion her way."

"But how did he get you to come here?" I asked, looking around the dark little room.

"I got a note that said someone would give me information about my father's death. I was to meet Uncle Phillip in the portrait gallery. He led me to the priest hole. And when I wasn't looking, he struck me down."

"Then he must have returned to leave me the note."

"Yes." Edward took my hand. "But that's enough talk. We are safe now. Let's leave this place."

The days that followed were busy ones. Uncle Phillip was taken away. Cousin Julia, content that the old earl's killer had been brought to justice, gave up trying to contact the spirits.

When quarter day arrived, Robert returned to London. But in two weeks time he was back, announcing that he meant to make his home in Cornwall with his joyful sons.

The boys have become the best of friends and have promised to look out for their new little sister/cousin.

Yes, God has blessed us with a new little life, a sweet girl baby with Edward's dark hair and eyes. Cousin Julia dotes on her and has become almost a new woman because of the child.

The castle has become the place of laughter and joy that I once hoped to make it. And Edward and I give thanks for a family that is now truly united by love.